T0002483

Risky

Shooting Stars Series

Fighting to Breathe
Wide-Open Spaces
One Last Wish

Underground Kings Series

Assumption
Obligation
Distraction
Infatuation

Ruby Falls Series

Falling Fast
One More Time

Fluke My Life Series

Running into Love
Stumbling into Love
Tossed into Love
Drawn into Love

How to Catch an Alpha Series

Catching Him
Baiting Him
Hooking Him

Stand-Alone Novels

Love at the Bluebird
The Wrong/Right Man
Alpha Law (written as C. A. Rose)
Justified (written as C. A. Rose)
Liability (written as C. A. Rose)
Finders Keepers (written as C. A. Rose)

To Have to Hold to Keep Series

Trapping Her
Taking Her (coming soon)
Stalking Her (coming soon)

Adventures in Love Series

Rushed

Risky

Adventures in Love, Book Two

AURORA ROSE REYNOLDS

 Montlake

This is a work of fiction. Names, characters, organizations, places, events, and incidents are either products of the author's imagination or are used fictitiously.

Text copyright © 2022 by Aurora Rose Reynolds
All rights reserved.

No part of this book may be reproduced, or stored in a retrieval system, or transmitted in any form or by any means, electronic, mechanical, photocopying, recording, or otherwise, without express written permission of the publisher.

Published by Montlake, Seattle

www.apub.com

Amazon, the Amazon logo, and Montlake are trademarks of Amazon.com, Inc., or its affiliates.

ISBN-13: 9781542034838
ISBN-10: 1542034833

Cover design by Hang Le

Cover photography by Regina Wamba of MaeIDesign.com

Printed in the United States of America

To my boys. I love you more than anything, and I'm forever grateful for you.

Chapter 1

EVERLY

I sit at the island in my parents' kitchen and smile as I listen to my mom talk to my ten-month-old son, Sampson, who babbles back to her in baby excitement. I know all parents think their kid is the smartest and the cutest, but Sampson really is both of those things. He's already started walking and using a few words and is adorable, with chubby cheeks, blond wavy hair, and big blue eyes that match my mom's and mine.

"I can't get over how big he's gotten the last three months." Mom's gaze comes to me, and Sampson gurgles his agreement, showing off his two bottom teeth that popped out last week.

"I told you."

"I know, but even in the pictures you sent, he still looked so tiny." She hefts his booty higher up onto her hip, then looks down at him. "What do you say you and I go out and track down Grandpa so Mama can unpack?"

"Mama," he repeats, turning to look at me, then holds out his chubby arms in my direction. Recognizing the sleepy look in his eyes, I scoot off the stool I'm sitting on and walk around to take him from my mom. As soon as I have ahold of him, he rests his cheek against my shoulder, and I palm the back of his head.

"It actually might be time for a nap. He didn't sleep much in the car on the way here," I tell her, and she touches his soft cheek with the tips of her fingers.

"Do you want me to make him a bottle?" she asks, and I nod, then watch her go to the fridge to get out the milk.

As she fills up a bottle, I rock my boy from side to side, the action a natural movement since the day he was born, something that seemed to be ingrained in me subconsciously. "I was thinking that tomorrow, if you don't mind watching Sampson, I might go out and put in my application at a few places around town."

"Already?" She stops on her way to the microwave and looks at me over her shoulder. "You don't want to take a week to settle in?"

"I'd rather hit the ground running, especially since it might take a couple of weeks to actually find something." I tip my head down to kiss the top of Sampson's head when he presses his face into my neck.

"You know your dad and I will always help you." Her voice is quiet, and the look in her eyes makes my chest hurt.

"I know, but you and Dad are already helping me out in a big way by letting us live here and for agreeing to watch Sampson while I work, when I *do* find a job."

"You're our daughter, and Sam is our grandson, Everly." She rolls her eyes at me like my last comment was ridiculous. "We're happy you're here and happy to help."

I know she and my dad are, and I'm so grateful for that, but none of this was part of my plan. I never thought I'd be in a situation where I'd be living at home with my parents again. I for sure never thought I'd be moving home with a baby, and I definitely didn't plan on being a single mom with an uninvolved baby daddy.

Two years ago, I met the man of my dreams, a guy named Lex, who was everything I wanted in a partner. He was well spoken, sweet, and a hard worker. Head over heels in love, I tied my rope to his star and followed him across the state to where he worked as a foreman for a construction company. Things were great—not just between Lex and me, but life in general was good. I had an awesome job managing one of the hotels in the city. I made some friends, and Lex started hinting at proposing.

I was happy.

We were happy.

Then I found out I was pregnant, and even though I knew it was soon, I thought everything would be okay. Only I was wrong . . . so very wrong. The moment I surprised Lex with a tiny baby onesie and my positive pregnancy test, he made a joke about me getting an abortion—which I laughed off, not wanting to believe he was serious. I thought he was just scared about becoming a dad, which I got, because the idea of becoming a mom freaked me out. I also knew I was already attached to the life growing inside me.

As the days turned into months and my belly grew, things between Lex and me became more and more strained. Even though we were still physically together, I felt as if I were alone. He wasn't open to me sharing anything about the pregnancy with him; he never talked about the baby or asked questions.

Still not wanting to be wrong about the man I'd fallen in love with, I was holding out hope that he would come around once Sampson was born. I thought maybe once he saw his son and held him, he would feel the connection I did and fall in love.

That didn't happen.

Instead, he started working more and sometimes stayed out all night. More than once, he came home smelling like perfume, and a few times, I would see texts from women pop up on his phone. Eventually, my heart couldn't take any more, and I told him I was leaving. He didn't ask me to stay. He didn't put up a fight. In fact, he helped me pack. Then this morning, he got me and my son in my car and sent us on our way.

"Everly," Mom calls, and I come out of my thoughts and blink my eyes open. "Are you okay?"

"Yeah." I take the bottle she's holding out to me. "Just spaced out."

"Are you tired?" Her eyes wander over my face. "Do you want me to take Sampson so you can sleep for a bit?"

"I think I'll just lie down with him." I hold Sampson a little tighter. For the last ten months, he's been all my responsibility, so thinking about doing something like just taking a nap while even *my mom* looks after him makes me feel anxious.

"Well then, while you do that, I'm going to take your dad some lunch and see what I can come up with for dinner."

"Sounds good. I'll be back down to help you cook." I turn to head for the doorway in the kitchen to take Sampson upstairs.

"Everly."

I stop to look at her over my shoulder and watch her shake her head while her eyes start to mist with tears.

"You're not alone anymore, honey." She clears her throat while placing her hand against her chest. "I know you've been doing this all by yourself, but you're not alone now."

With my throat getting tight, I nod and leave the kitchen before I break down in tears. For so long, I didn't tell anyone what was happening between Lex and me, because I was positive things would get better, and I didn't want anyone to have animosity toward him when they did. Now, I wish I would have opened up about everything, at least to my mom. I could have used her advice and support, especially when I didn't have anyone.

When I get upstairs, I walk past my brother Jayson's room, which had been empty for years and is now Sampson's nursery—courtesy of my mom and her friends—and head for my bedroom, at the end of the hall. With Sampson starting to fuss, I get comfortable on my bed before giving him his bottle, then watch him with wonder as he eats.

I grew up in a house filled with love and have been lucky to experience love a time or two in my life, but I never really knew how fully I could love another person until I gave birth to the baby in my arms. In such a short time, he's taught me so much about myself and what really matters in life.

Once he's finished eating, I rest him against my shoulder and burp him, then hold him until he falls asleep. As he drifts off, I silently promise him that I will always make him a priority and that there will never be a day in which he thinks he's not wanted.

～

Lying on the floor with Sampson, I grab him up before he can climb over my stomach and then start to tickle him. I smile when I hear him laugh, and I sit up with him in my arms when my cell starts to ring. I take him with me across the room, grab my phone, and try not to get my hopes up when I recognize the number on the screen. I've been at my parents' now for three weeks, and in that time, I've applied to at least a hundred places and have gone through a dozen interviews, but I have yet to get a job offer.

"Hello?" I answer, putting my cell to my ear.

"Everly, it's Maverick from Live Life Adventures." When Sampson starts to fuss, wanting to get down, Maverick adds, "Is this a good time?"

"Hi, Maverick. Yes, now is fine. How are things?" I place Sampson on the ground, and he immediately starts to crawl to where his toys are.

"Things are good. I wanted to reach out to you to see if you're still interested in managing the office here at the lodge."

"Are you kidding? Of course I'm still interested!" I blurt out, then cringe, realizing how unprofessional I sound. "Sorry. I mean yes, I'm still interested."

"Good." He chuckles. "Do you have time tomorrow or the next day to come in, meet with me and Tanner to go over a few things, and fill out some paperwork?"

"Absolutely. Just tell me when, and I'll be there," I assure him, knowing I probably sound far too excited, but honestly I *am* excited. I need money, which means I need a job.

"Great, well, if tomorrow works for you, let's meet after lunch . . . say around three."

"Sure! Awesome. That sounds great. I'll be there."

"See you then, Everly." He hangs up after a quick goodbye, and as soon as I know the call has ended, I jump up and down.

"I think I got a job!" I shout and clap, startling Sampson, who was standing and holding a ball. He falls to his bottom and immediately begins to cry. "Oh no, sorry, baby." I rush to pick him up. "Mommy is just happy; I didn't mean to scare you." I kiss his squishy cheek and wipe away his tears.

"Is everything okay?" Mom asks, coming into the living room, and I grin at her.

"Yeah, I just got off the phone with Maverick from Live Life Adventures, and he wants me to come in tomorrow to talk and fill out paperwork. I got so excited that I scared Sampson when I got off the phone."

"So you got the job?" She walks toward me when Sampson reaches out for her.

"I think so. I mean, he didn't say that I did, but he did ask if I was still interested and wants to meet, so I think so."

"That's great, sweetheart."

"Right?" I watch her take Sampson to where his pile of blocks is and start to play with him. "It'll be nice to have some money coming in again."

"Have you talked to Lex about helping you out?" Her eyes come to me, and I shift on my feet, feeling uncomfortable.

"I don't want anything from him."

"I know you don't," she says quietly, then continues: "But this isn't about you. It's about Sampson. And even if he doesn't want to be a part of Sampson's life, he should still help out, don't you think?"

"No," I say softly, picking up one of Sampson's stuffed animals and holding it while I take a seat on the couch. "He never hid the fact that he didn't want to be a dad, and even though it sucks, I'm not sure I should hold him responsible."

"Everly—"

"Mom, please." I grip the stuffed animal tighter. "I know you feel differently about the situation, but at the end of the day, it's my choice."

"You're right." She sighs, sounding disappointed. I get it. I understand why she's disappointed in the situation between Lex and me, but the truth is, he made it clear where he stood from the beginning, and I have to respect that. I also know he's proven he doesn't care about Sampson or me. I have only spoken to him one time since I've been here, and that was over texts, where I told him that I arrived safely, and he messaged me back with a simple Good in response.

"So do you think you can watch Sampson tomorrow?" I change the subject, because if I do overthink things with Lex, I'll end up getting angry, sad, or disappointed, and none of those things are good for my mental health.

"You already know I can."

"Thanks, Mom."

"Anytime, honey." She reaches over to rub the top of my knee, then looks across the room when the back door opens and my dad walks in. Like always when she sees my father, a light fills her eyes that is solely reserved for him. Even after thirty-plus years of being married, they're still just as grossly affectionate and in love as I remember them being when I was growing up. Not that they don't bicker and drive each other crazy, but they definitely have more good times than bad and always make their relationship a priority.

"What are you two in here talking about?" Dad asks as he walks into the room, and as soon as Sampson hears his voice, he immediately gets up and waddles over to Dad. He picks him up, then lifts him above his head to blow against his belly.

"Everly got a job," Mom says, going to Dad and snagging a kiss.

"Hopefully," I cut in, and Dad looks at me. "I have to go meet with Maverick and Tanner at the Live Life Adventures Lodge tomorrow to talk about stuff."

"That's great news, and they'd be dumb not to hire you."

"Dumb, dumb, dumb, dumb." Sampson pats Dad's beard-covered cheek, laughing, and I groan.

"Dad."

"At least it's not shi—"

"Don't say it," I say, cutting him off, because Sampson has reached the age of repeating, and even though he has no idea what he's saying, and most of the time you can hardly understand him, I don't really relish the idea of my sweet, adorable baby boy walking around spouting curse words all day.

"I wasn't going to say it," Dad says with a grin, and I roll my eyes, because he is so full of it. He curses all the time—so much so that he doesn't even recognize when he's doing it. "I just came to see if you or your mom would mind coming to the office to answer the phone and hang out for an hour or so while I run out to meet a client, in case anyone stops by."

"Is Sandy still out sick?" Mom asks, and he gives her a look.

"You know she's not sick. You're the one who showed me the pictures of her out on the lake with her boy toy yesterday."

"I didn't actually mean *sick*." Mom rolls her eyes. "I mean, did she call out again today?"

"She did but assured me that she would be back tomorrow." Dad smiles, not looking even a little upset; then it clicks who they're talking about.

"Wait," I cut in with a frown. "Are you two talking about Miss Sandy, who started working for you a few months ago?" I ask, trying to remember details about her, but all that comes to mind is her long gray hair and tan wrinkly skin.

"We are," Mom confirms.

"She has a boyfriend?"

"She does. A while back, she met a guy on the internet, and whenever he's in town, she plays hooky from work to spend time with him."

"How old is she?"

"Sixty-seven, I think," Dad says, passing Sampson over to Mom.

"Wow. Well, good for her," I reply, impressed.

"So can either of you come over to the office?" Dad looks between us. "I won't be out long."

"I don't mind, unless you want to go." I look to my mom, and she shakes her head immediately, which doesn't surprise me.

My dad owns a small law office, which is located just down the block. When he first opened his practice, Mom tried working for him but learned quickly that it wasn't a fit. I get it, because there is no way I could work for my dad either. It's not that he's a bad boss; it's just that he has a way of doing things that doesn't make much sense to anyone else.

"Are you good with Sampson, or do you want me to take him with me?"

"He can stay here with Grandma." Mom kisses Sampson's cheek.

"Cool, I just need to change and brush my hair."

"You look fine, and what you have on is okay," Dad says, and I look down at my baggy T-shirt and sweats that both have spots on them from Sampson's breakfast this morning, along with drool and Lord knows what else.

"You think this is appropriate?" I hold the fabric away from my body and raise a brow at my father. Then I hear my mom sigh when he shrugs.

"You look all right to me."

"Well, thank you, Dad, for your seal of approval, but I think I'm going to put on something that is not covered in drool." I laugh, giving Sampson a kiss before I head upstairs.

Before becoming a mom, I never realized how much I took getting dressed for granted. It's not that I don't still get dressed every day, but most days, I don't have a reason to wear anything besides sweats and baggy T-shirts, things that are comfortable for rolling around on the floor or chasing after Sampson. After deciding on a pair of dark jeans, I roll up the bottoms to show off my brown wedge boots, then grab my favorite thick sweater from my closet. The color is not quite peach and not quite pink. I tuck the front into the top of my jeans to make it look more formfitting and add a belt that matches my boots.

Now dressed, I go to the bathroom and run a brush through my long dark hair and decide to put on some makeup—another thing that is a rarity most days. When I'm done, I meet my dad downstairs, and after giving Sampson one more kiss, I grab my coat and hat, then head outside with my dad.

"Here's the key." Dad pulls the key from the front pocket of his jeans that are almost the same color as mine and places it in my hand.

"Is there anyone you're expecting to stop by today?" I ask, trying to take my mind off the cold wind that's beginning to make my cheeks burn.

"Not before I get back." He glances up at the sky as snow starts to fall, then down the block. "Do you want me to drive you?"

"No, I could use the walk," I tell him, and he nods.

"Call if you need me."

"Will do." I give him a salute that makes him smile, then start down the sidewalk when I hear him get into his car behind me. When we moved here my junior year of high school, I always thought it was so cool that we lived in town. Where other kids would have to convince their parents to drop them off to shop, go see a movie, or have dinner,

I just had to walk out my front door and head down the street. Now that I'm older, I still feel the same way, and I can't wait for the weather to warm up so I can put Sampson in his stroller and spend the day wandering around town with him.

It only takes a couple of minutes to make it to the office on Main Street—something I'm thankful for when the wind picks up and snow starts to fall harder. After I get inside, I turn the OUT TO LUNCH sign around, take off my jacket and hat, and flip on the lights. Dad's office is small, consisting of just three rooms: the entry—which has a desk facing the front door, along with a small couch and coffee station set up for clients—a restroom, and my dad's office, which is at the back.

Figuring I should be in the front in case someone does come in, I make myself comfortable at Sandy's desk, and a stained glass–framed photo next to the computer catches my eye. I pick it up to get a better look and spot Sandy with her gray hair and wide smile, standing in the middle of a large group of happy-looking people, and I wonder if it's her family.

As I scan the photo more closely, a really good-looking guy with blondish hair snags my attention. Biting my lip, I wonder who he is, then glance up when the door to the office is opened. I gasp when the guy I was just staring at steps into the office like I conjured him up. I'm stunned by his presence, and the frame in my hands slips through my fingers and sounds like it shatters when it hits the ground. I panic, bending quickly to pick it up, then cry out when I hit my forehead on the edge of the desk with enough force that I see stars.

"Shit," the guy says as I cover my forehead with my hand and roll the chair back into the wall behind me, barely catching myself before I tumble out of the chair. "Easy." His warm hand takes hold of my wrist, and a zing shoots up my arm. I blink my eyes open as my hand is tugged away, and my heart starts to race as our eyes meet and I see him frowning at me.

"I'm okay." I try to tug my wrist from his grasp, but his hold is firm as beautiful sea-green eyes scan my face.

"You're not bleeding," he says quietly as his other hand comes up, and his thumb smooths over my forehead, causing a shiver to slide down my spine. "But you're going to have a bump if you don't put some ice on this." He lets me go, and I'm oddly disappointed when he steps back, taking his warmth and scent with him, then beyond confused when he heads for the door and walks out without another word.

"Did that just happen?" I blink at the empty space he was just standing in, the headache I feel coming on the only reason I know I'm not dreaming. With a shake of my head, I start to carefully pick up the broken pieces of glass from the frame, which I hope isn't a priceless family heirloom but from one of the shops here in town.

Just when I've gotten all of it cleaned up and the photo tucked away, someone knocks on the office door right before it opens again.

"I didn't want to startle you again." The guy from before steps inside, holding a small white bag in one hand and a cup in the other.

"Oh." I try to think of something more to say as he places the cup and bag on the side of the desk and slips off his jacket, leaving him in a green thermal that's molded to his fit torso.

"Have a seat," he orders, motioning to the chair next to me while opening the bag and pulling out a small bottle of pain reliever and a piece of fabric. As he takes the lid off the cup, dumps a handful of ice onto the piece of cloth, and twists the end, I wonder if I really am dreaming. "Babe." His gaze meets mine, and I open and close my mouth like a fish out of water, trying to get my brain and mouth to work in unison. "Please sit."

I stumble to the chair and sit, then watch him prowl around the side of the desk to me. *How didn't I notice before how big he is?* Not only is he tall, but his shoulders are wide enough for me to fit between them twice. His legs are the size of tree trunks, and he looks like he could bench-press me without breaking a sweat, and I'm not a tiny girl.

Risky

"Hold this to your head while I get you some water." He gently places the ice pack against my forehead, then lifts my hand to take over, like I'm a helpless child.

"You didn't have to do this," I tell him quietly as he goes to the small fridge under the coffee station and pulls out a bottle of water.

"It happened because of me." He comes back to the desk, picks up the bottle of pills, and starts reading the back.

"I'm pretty sure it happened because I'm a klutz."

"Yeah." His eyes meet mine, and I watch in fascination as his lips tip up into a small smirk that does funny things to my stomach. In the photo, I could see he was good looking, but seeing the sharpness of his scruff-covered jaw, along with his gorgeous eyes and full lips up close and personal, takes him to a whole other level of handsome. "The bottle says to take two, but I think one should work." He opens the bottle and shakes out one small white pill, handing it to me before screwing off the lid to the water and passing it over.

"Thanks." I take it from him and swallow the pill down with a gulp of water.

"No problem." He studies me as he crosses his arms over his chest, making his biceps seem even larger. "I'm guessing, since you're here and my grandmother isn't, you're covering for her today."

"Sandy?" I ask, and he lifts his chin in an affirmation. "She called out sick."

"Sick . . . right," he mutters, and I press my lips together, because it's obvious he knows where she is and isn't happy about it. "I should have called her cell before I stopped by."

"Sorry."

"Not your fault." He sighs, then takes a seat on the edge of the desk and scrubs his hands down his face.

"Is there something I can do to help?"

"Can you make my family act normal for once?"

"Probably not."

13

"Didn't think so." He sighs again, stands up, and grabs his jacket. "I didn't catch your name."

"Oh." I lick my lips. "Everly."

"Blake."

"Nice to meet you."

"You too." He puts on his coat, then pulls a winter cap out of his pocket and puts it on. "So are you just helping out here today, or is Gene firing my grandmother, who's been acting like she's sixteen again?"

"My dad isn't firing your grandma."

"You're Gene's daughter?" His brows draw together slightly. "The one with the kid?"

"That's me," I mumble, unsure what to make of his look.

"Cool." He tucks his hands into the front pockets of his jeans. "I'm gonna head out, but make sure you keep ice on your head."

"Will do," I agree, watching him walk out. When the door closes behind him, I stare at it for longer than I should while trying to figure out why I feel so disappointed.

Chapter 2

BLAKE

After I pull up to the Live Life Adventures Lodge, I put my truck in park, then grab my cell when it starts to ring. Seeing my dad is calling, I slide my finger across the screen and put it to my ear.

"Hey, Dad."

"Hey, kid. You good?"

"Yeah, what's up? You okay?" The question is ridiculous, given that we both know he's not okay, but this has been my life for the last year, pretending that everything is fine when it's not.

"Yeah." He clears his throat. "Just wanted to let you know that I'm going to need you to cover for me this week."

"Sure." I rub my chest in a pointless attempt to get rid of the ache there. "Are your appointments the same time as last week?"

"A little later in the afternoons."

"Will you be all right driving yourself?"

"I'll be fine," he says quickly, and I shake my head, not sure that he would tell me even if he wasn't going to be fine. I always knew my father was stubborn, but until recently I didn't know just how stubborn he could be.

"You know I'm here for whatever you need."

"I know." He lets out a long breath. "Love you, kid. We'll talk soon."

"Love you, too, Dad." I hang up and tap my phone against my thigh. When my dad first confided in me about his prostate cancer diagnosis, I felt like my world was coming to an end. I grew up thinking of him as invincible, thinking that no matter what, he would always be around. The realization that not only is he human but that my time with him is limited was devastating. Then he asked me to keep the truth a secret; he didn't want my mom or sister to worry, and given how I was feeling, I agreed to help hide the truth from them. Now, months later, I'm not sure that was the right decision. So far his doctors are hopeful that the proton therapy he's doing is working and the side effects are minimal, which is great, but I don't know that it's healthy for him to continue going through this alone. And I don't know that I'm strong enough to carry this burden alone any longer.

With a sigh, I send a text to my sister and another to my mom to just check in. Even if they don't know what's happening, it makes me feel better knowing they're both okay. Once I'm done, I respond to the string of texts waiting for me, then get out of my truck and head up the steps into the lodge. I'm already exhausted and the day hasn't even started. Between my dad, my family, work, and life in general, it feels like I have no time for myself, and that's not going to change anytime soon. In two days, we have a group of ten people coming in for a weeklong company retreat, so I want to double-check that everything is ready to go, even though both Maverick and Tanner, who co-own the business with me, have said more than once that we're ready for our guests.

Logically, I know I can trust the two of them to handle things. For years while we were in the military together, they were the ones I depended on to keep me safe, and vice versa. I just have a hard time letting go of control, and now more than ever, I need to make sure we keep turning a profit, especially since I'm the one paying for my dad's cancer treatments after his insurance refused to cover any of the cost.

As I head for the office, I hear the sound of a woman laughing, and I frown, not recognizing it. There are only three women who are constants around the lodge—my mother, my sister, Margret, and Cybil, Tanner's wife—and none of them are here today.

When I get to the office at the end of the hall, I walk inside and stop dead in my tracks. Sitting around the only desk in the room are Tanner, Maverick . . . and Everly. Everly, the pretty brunette I met yesterday at Gene's office—the *really* fucking pretty brunette, who is totally off-limits, since she's got a man and a kid.

"What's going on here?" I ask, and all eyes in the room come to me, two sets filled with guilt, one set with a hell of a lot of surprise.

"Everly just accepted the office-manager job, so we're going over the schedule for the week," Mav says as he leans back in his chair.

"We figured it would be good to get her on board before our next group shows up," Tanner adds, and my spine stiffens.

"I need to talk to you two outside." I watch Mav and Tanner share a look before they both stand.

"We'll be right back," I hear Mav tell Everly softly as I walk out of the room with Tanner right behind me.

Trying to breathe through the irrational anger and frustration I'm feeling, I head through the lodge and out the front door. I know we need to hire someone, but again, it's difficult for me to give up control, so I want to make sure we pick the right person.

When I get down the steps of the front porch, I turn on two of the men I love like family and bite out, "What the fuck?"

"We told you we needed to hire someone." Mav shrugs casually, which is his way. The guy has always acted cool as a cucumber. Even if he's pissed, you'd never know. "We interviewed over forty people, and you—"

"Not one of those candidates was cut out to work here, and you know it," I say, cutting him off before he can finish speaking.

"Some of those people were overqualified to work here, and *you* know it," Tanner replies, crossing his arms over his chest, and I drag in a deep breath. He's right; some of the people we interviewed were overqualified, but none of them were the right fit.

"I know it's difficult for you to trust people and to let go of control, but we need to hire someone, and Everly is perfect for the job," Mav says, his expression softening on her name, and irrational jealousy curls up in the pit of my stomach.

"She's got a man and a kid. You know that, right?" I say with a clenched jaw, and he raises a brow.

"What does that have to do with anything?"

"Nothing." And it doesn't have anything to do with her being able to work here, but there is no denying that the idea of one of my best friends possibly having feelings for her bothers the fuck out of me, when it shouldn't.

"Do you know her?" Tanner asks, and I rip my fingers through my hair.

"No. Yes, I met her yesterday at Gene's. She's his daughter, and my grandmother mentioned she has a kid and a man."

"Hmm." He smirks, and I narrow my eyes on him.

"What?"

"Nothing." He lets his arms fall to his sides and shakes his head. "We can't continue to put this off, is all I'm going to say. Cybil is gonna need me after she has the baby, and I want to be home with my wife and kid for at least a few weeks, if not longer."

"I know that," I say quietly, wanting that for him, too, knowing how important it is that I support his decision after the way I reacted to his relationship in the past. When he and Cybil first hooked up last summer, I was pissed and let it show. Cybil had come to Montana for one of our couples retreats alone after her fiancé ended their engagement.

During that time, with Tanner as her partner, they had gotten close. So close that she decided to extend her visit and stay with him, and then he followed her home to Oregon when the woman who helped raise her had a heart attack. I wish I could go back and change how I reacted to them falling in love, but the truth is, I was afraid I was going to lose one of my best friends right after my father confided in me about having cancer, which he didn't want anyone to know about.

"We know you don't want someone stepping in at the last minute, and yeah, we shouldn't have agreed to hire Everly without you, but we knew you'd find something wrong with her too," Mav says, and my jaw clenches. I want to say he doesn't know what he's talking about, but he and Tanner both know me better than anyone.

"Does she even know how to ride a four-wheeler, clean fish, change a tire?" I ask, grasping at straws, because the chance of her having to do any of those things is very unlikely.

"No, but she can learn." Mav shrugs, then adds, "The important thing is she knows how to run an office. The rest, we can teach her how to do if it's necessary. We just need you to be nice and to not scare her off."

"I'm not going to scare her off."

"Right." Tanner presses his lips together. "You stomping into the office and acting like a growling beast really gave the impression that you're someone who'd make a great boss."

"I wasn't a growling beast."

"You were." We all turn at that comment from Everly to find her standing at the top of the stairs with her shoulder resting against the post and her arms crossed over her chest. Her posture is casual, but the hint of annoyance in her expression makes me wonder how long she's been there. "But it's okay. I get it now that you were caught off guard."

"He didn't know we hired you," Tanner tells her, and she dips her chin slightly; then her gaze meets mine.

"I know you don't know me, and I'm aware you have some issue with the fact that I have a kid, but me being a mother is the reason I'm the best person for this job. As a single mom, I need a stable income in order to provide the best life for my son, and in order to get that income, I need to work. That means I will show up when I'm scheduled and do everything in my power to keep working here, and if you give me a chance, you won't be disappointed."

"I don't have an issue with you having a kid." I zero in on that comment, trying not to think about why I'm so relieved that she said she's single, and she tips her head to the side and shrugs one shoulder like she doesn't believe me.

"You've brought up me being a mom twice now and acted weird about it each time," she says, coming down the steps to where we're standing.

"I never acted weird about it, and it's rude to eavesdrop, you know."

"Maybe," she agrees, and damn if there isn't something about her attitude that is so attractive.

"Well, as entertaining as this is, I need to go," Tanner says, patting me on the shoulder. "Cybil's checkup is in an hour, and I'm meeting her at the doctor's office before I head out to meet the guys delivering the gas to the tank on the back of the property."

"Sure," I reply. "Is dinner still on for tomorrow?"

"You know it," he says, then looks at Everly. "If you're not doing anything tomorrow evening around five, you're welcome to join us, and bring your son. We normally get together for dinner at my place before and after we have a big group come in."

"Oh." She glances at me quickly. "Thanks for the offer, but I'm not sure I'll be able to make it."

"Don't let this grump be the reason you don't join us." Mav claps me on the back, and she smiles, making her prettiness even prettier.

"I'll think about it," she agrees as my cell starts to ring. I pull it out of my pocket, and when I see it's my dad calling, I take a step back from the group.

"Sorry, I gotta take this." I turn and head up the stairs while putting my cell to my ear, all thoughts of Everly, her smile, and the fact that she's single taking a back seat to my current reality.

Chapter 3

EVERLY

After yawning for the third time in a row, I push away from my desk and head out of my office. The closer I get to the kitchen, the stronger the scent of freshly brewed coffee gets. Sampson has been keeping me up the last couple of nights, and that, mixed with having a job I have to get up for and be at early, means I'm exhausted.

I reach the kitchen and pause in the doorway when I see a woman mixing something in a large metal bowl. Maverick and Tanner both told me that Blake's mom, Janet, runs the kitchen when we have guests, but I haven't met her yet.

I shift on my feet as I debate turning around and heading back to the office, coffee seeming less important than it did a few minutes ago. For whatever reason, Blake isn't my biggest fan, and I'm not sure if he's shared his dislike for me with his mom.

"I don't bite." I focus on the woman across the room at that comment and watch her smile warmly. "You must be Everly."

"I am, and you're Janet?" I prompt, and she nods.

"That's me." She motions to the coffeepot on the counter with a tip of her head. "Coffee's fresh, and if you don't mind being a guinea pig and aren't allergic to gluten or on a diet, I've got some fresh apple pie scones coming out of the oven in just a few minutes."

"I love carbs, and diets are dumb."

"A woman after my own heart." She laughs, and the tension in my shoulders eases. "Get yourself a cup of coffee and pull up a stool," she orders, and I don't put up an argument. After filling a mug, I dump in some cream and sugar and take a seat across from her at a long metal island in the middle of the massive industrial kitchen.

"So tell me about yourself," she says as I take my first sip of heaven in a cup.

"There isn't much to tell you," I reply, and she stops what she's doing to study me.

"We both know that's a lie. I can tell just by looking into your eyes that you've got a story."

"True, but my story can't fit into the next fifteen minutes," I tell her quietly, and her expression softens.

"Fair enough. Tell me the good parts then."

"I have a son," I start. "His name is Sampson, and he just turned eleven months old."

"Do you have any pictures?"

"On my phone, I have a million, but I left my cell in the office when I smelled the coffee brewing in here."

"Then you have a reason to come back and visit me again." She smiles before dumping a bag of pecans into the bowl she's been mixing.

"What are you making?"

"Chicken fruit salad," she tells me, and I must make a face, because she laughs.

"It's delicious. Give me a second to finish up, and I'll give you a bite."

"That's not necessary." I shake my head and hold up a hand.

"Do you like chicken?"

"Yes."

"Grapes, pineapple, pecans?" she asks as she grabs a couple of spices and sprinkles them into the bowl.

"Yes."

"Then you'll like it," she assures me as she begins mixing the contents of the bowl once more.

"I don't think so," I deny, and she grabs a fork from a drawer, then scoops up some of the salad and hands it over to me.

"Just try it."

Not wanting to be rude, I take the bite off the fork, and as I chew, I'm surprised how delicious the mixture is. The crunch from what I'm guessing is celery and pecans, along with the sweetness of pineapple and grapes and the spice of red onion, is like a party in my mouth.

"So what do you think?"

"Can I have the recipe?" I ask after I swallow, and the smile she gives me lights up her whole face.

"No, but I can make you a sandwich and leave it in the fridge so you can have it at lunch."

"That works, too," I say, and she takes the fork back and tosses it into the sink.

"So how are you liking working here?" Not sure I should tell her that I love working here but that her son is kind of an ass, I shrug.

"I like it. I still have lots to learn, but I'm starting to realize that will all come with time."

"You're right about that. I had a huge learning curve when I decided to take over the kitchen." She walks to the double ovens on the wall when an alarm dings and puts on oven mitts before she pulls out a tray of golden scones that look like they should be in a magazine. "They look good." She slips one off the tray and onto a plate. "I just need you to tell me if they taste good."

With the plate in front of me, I pull off a piece and blow across it before tossing it into my mouth. As I savor the bite of sweet bread, apples, and spices, I shake my head before I swallow. "If I ever hit the lottery, I'm stealing you away from this place and hiring you myself."

"I might just take you up on that offer," she says; then her eyes move over my shoulder as an odd sensation travels up my spine. Turning on my stool, I watch Blake walk into the kitchen and head around the island I'm sitting at to kiss his mom on the cheek. Seeing that from him and the happy look on her face, I relax. For the last couple of days, I've started to wonder if I've been avoiding him or if he's been avoiding me. All I know is we haven't spent much—if any—time together, and when we are in the same vicinity, we each avoid any type of interaction.

"It smells good in here," he tells her, starting to pick up one of the scones, and she smacks his hand.

"Those are for guests," she tells him, and he looks at the plate sitting in front of me.

"You gave one to Everly."

"That's because she was my tester. Now that I know they're good enough for the clients, they're for the clients," she tells him, and he pouts his bottom lip.

If any other man did that, I would find it ridiculously immature, but him doing it is somehow adorable.

"You can have the rest of this one," I say, pushing the plate in front of me across the island, and he looks down at it before meeting my gaze. One look shouldn't have the ability to make my pulse skitter and a few places on my body tingle, but unfortunately, it's exactly what happens when he looks at me. That's when I know I need to go and that I need to continue avoiding him as much as possible. The last thing I need is to develop a crush on a guy who's as approachable as a grizzly and as prickly as a cactus.

"Thanks for letting me hang with you," I tell Janet as I stand with my coffee, and her gaze pings between Blake and me before she focuses on me.

"You're welcome in my kitchen anytime, and don't forget to come back at lunch to get your sandwich. If I'm not here, it will be in the fridge."

"I definitely won't forget, and thank you again," I say before I hustle out of the kitchen, trying to look like I'm not running away. When I get back to the office, I step inside and smile when I see Maverick sitting at what is now my desk. Where Blake is unapproachable and prickly, Maverick is open and friendly. That being said, I don't think we're friends yet, and I have the feeling it takes a lot for him to trust people and let them in.

"Hey," he says as I set my cup of coffee on the desk, and he drops his eyes to my mug. "Did you meet Janet?"

"I did. She's sweet," I say as he rolls back from the desk and stands.

"She is," he agrees, motioning for me to go sit in the chair he just vacated, so I scoot around him and take a seat. "How are you feeling after the last couple of days?"

"Good. I mean, I've got the booking process down, and answering emails and phone calls is easy. The rest is going to take me a while to learn."

"You have time, and you know you can call any one of us if you ever have questions."

"I know. Tanner helped me yesterday when I was stuck trying to figure out some of the verbiage you guys use for ordering supplies, then told me that the only way to get the copy machine to work is to kick it in just the right spot." He laughs. As he does, I enjoy the show. He might not make my pulse race, but that doesn't mean he's not attractive. Like Tanner and Blake, he's a really good-looking man, and even more so with his dark, almost black hair, regal features, and tan skin.

"It's probably time we replace it."

"Replace what?" Blake asks, coming into the room, and once again, my stupid body reacts to his presence, making me annoyed with myself.

"The copy machine," Maverick tells him as he takes a seat across from me, settling in like he owns the place, which I guess he kinda does. It's also weird that he's in here, because he hasn't been in here since I started working.

"Yeah, we should get a new one. We bought it used from a mailing place in town that was going out of business. It's great when it works like it should but a pain in the ass when it doesn't."

"It's also a waste to spend money on paper and ink when most people nowadays can download an app on their cell phone," I say, and all of his attention comes to me as he frowns.

"That won't work if we're out in the middle of nowhere without electricity."

"An app might not work all the time, but I noticed the safety information, schedules, maps, and stuff are recycled for each group. So I could laminate the sheets that go out with the guests, then take them back when the week is over to save on having to print them for each group that comes in."

"That's smart. If you have time today, check out how much a laminating machine is, and let us know," Maverick says.

"Or I could just take the printouts to town and have someone laminate them. It probably won't cost much."

"How about we test out your idea with the bachelor/bachelorette party that's coming in the week after next and see if it's worth the cost," Blake says, and I blink at him.

"Did you just say a bachelor/bachelorette party is coming here?"

"It's on the schedule," Maverick says, and I shake my head before turning to the computer and pulling up the calendar, because I'm sure I would have remembered seeing that.

"It says *Bach party*," I tell the room. "I thought that was the name of the group."

"Nope," Maverick replies, and I look up at him, since he's still standing. "The couple who booked that party took part in one of our couples retreats last summer and are coming here with their friends for the weekend before their wedding."

"Wow, okay," I mutter. I mean, going out into the wilderness without a shower isn't my idea of a good time, but to each their own, right?

"Sounds fun," I lie, and Blake chuckles while Maverick looks at him like he's never heard him laugh before.

"We should get breakfast out to the group." Blake stands suddenly, and Maverick checks his watch before looking at me.

"After I drop Blake off, I'll be back. Do you want to have lunch then?"

"She needs to be here to answer the phone," Blake says before I can open my mouth to respond, and Maverick turns slightly, raising a brow.

"We all get lunch."

"Whatever," Blake grumbles. "I gotta go."

When he leaves, I catch Maverick's lips tip up ever so slightly before he turns to face me, with the smile that was forming seconds ago now gone, like it didn't even exist.

"I just remembered that I have something to do today, so I won't be back until late. We'll get lunch another time."

"Yeah, sure," I mutter, and he lifts his chin before taking off. Since I know I won't be able to figure out what that was all about, I get to work, because at the end of the day, providing for Sampson is the reason I'm here.

Chapter 4

EVERLY

"Are you excited about tonight?" my mom asks as she comes into the kitchen, where I'm attempting to feed Sampson his lunch, even though he's more interested in making a mess with his spaghetti than actually eating it. It's Sunday, and yesterday, we said farewell to the group of guests who had been in for a weeklong retreat.

"A little," I tell her, scooping up another bite of noodles and using the airplane technique to urge him to take a bite. "It will be nice to meet Cybil, Tanner's wife, since I've heard so much about her, and fun to see Sampson with Taylor, Margret's daughter, since they're so close in age."

"I'm happy you're going to be making some friends."

"I have friends," I say, leaving out that I don't really have friends *here*, since I don't talk to most of the people I grew up with anymore, and the few who I do still talk to have moved away and started families of their own.

"I mean real-life friends, not online friends." Mom rolls her eyes. "And it'll be good for you to have other mom friends."

"I guess you're right."

"What about Mr. Grumpy Pants? Is he going to be there tonight?" she asks, and I know she's referring to Blake, since that's the name she made up for him after I told her about a few of our interactions, most of them including him grunting or grouching.

"I don't know, but I'm guessing yes," I reply, and she nods. The truth is, I've been seriously apprehensive about getting together with everyone outside of work. I probably would have said no to hanging out tonight, but both Tanner and Maverick laid on the guilt. And since they've been so nice to me, it didn't feel right telling them no, like I've done before.

"It's going to be great; I just know it." She smiles, and I smile back, hoping she's right.

~

This is so not great, I think to myself as I rock Sampson, who hasn't stopped crying for the last fifteen minutes. When we arrived at Tanner and Cybil's house—a house that is as beautiful on the outside as it is within—he was fine. He was his adorable self while meeting Tanner, Cybil, Maverick, Margret, and her daughter, Taylor, but then all hell broke loose. When he started to cry with no end in sight, I took up residence on the couch in the living room and haven't moved since then, except to give him some Tylenol, figuring it's his teeth that are bothering him.

Thankfully, with Margret having Taylor and Cybil being pregnant, there was nothing but understanding from the group as they went outside to the back porch to give us a little space.

"It's okay. You're okay." I kiss the top of his head and wonder if I should just call it a night and take him home. He's never this cranky unless he's not feeling great, and being in his own space might help calm him down.

Hearing the doorbell ring, I wait for someone to come inside to answer it, but when no one does and it rings again, I push up off the couch. I carry Sampson with me to the front door, then see Blake standing outside the glass, his eyes pointed down to his feet. Once I'm standing in front of it, his head lifts, his eyes meet mine, and, as always happens when it comes to him, my stupid hormones react.

"Hey," I say as I pull the door open, then gasp when a huge brown ball of fur lunges toward me, making a chuffing noise.

"Tutu, sit," Blake orders, and what can only be described as a bear falls to its bottom a foot in front of me with its whole giant body wagging.

With my heart now pounding for a different reason, I look down at the large animal, seeing it's not a bear but a giant fluffy dog. Seriously, it has to be the biggest dog I have ever seen in my life.

"I'm sorry about that." Blake takes a step into the house, shutting the door. "She normally doesn't do that."

"It's okay," I say over the sound of Sampson crying, and Blake eyes him, his brows dragging together.

"Sorry about her scaring him."

"She didn't. He's teething," I tell him, bouncing Sampson on my hip. "I think we might take off, since he's not feeling well."

"Hey, big guy," Blake says softly, touching Sampson's cheek, and my boy focuses on him and grabs hold of his finger, then reaches out for him, babbling something. "It's that bad, huh?" He takes hold of him, and since he's no longer crying, I let him go, watching as Blake holds him easily against his large chest. "He's cute," he tells me, and my heart feels weird.

"Thanks."

"Do you want to meet Tutu?" he asks Sampson, who immediately starts to shout, "Tutu! Tutu!"

"Be gentle, girl." Blake squats down in front of the pup, and I hold my breath as the dog wiggles forward on her bottom to sniff Sampson before licking his arm, making him squeal in baby excitement. "Good girl," Blake praises, and she lifts her paw to his knee.

"What kind of dog is she?" I ask, and he tips his head back to look at me.

"A Tibetan mastiff."

"She looks like a bear." I squat down next to Blake, then hold my hand out toward her, and she loses interest in Sampson and Blake, scooting closer to me. When she's in front of me, I use both my hands to scratch the fluff on her head. Her thick dark hair must be at least eight inches long and is so soft to the touch. "You're a sweet girl, aren't you?" I whisper, and she gets even closer, her heavy weight knocking me off-balance.

"Tutu," Blake calls as I fall on my ass, then laugh as she crawls over me to get to my face.

"It's okay." I take hold of her head in my hands and scoot back until I have room to sit up, then give her one more rubdown. When I can finally stand, I attempt to take Sampson back, but my boy is not even a little interested in me, and Blake seems more than content to hold him.

"Where is everyone?" he asks as he walks farther into the house.

"Outside."

"You're not hanging with them?" He turns to look at me, and I shrug.

"Sampson was crying, and I didn't want to ruin everyone else's good time."

"He seems okay now." He looks at Sampson, who takes that time to bop him on the side of the face with his tiny fist and babble something. "You want to go outside, big guy?" To that question, Sampson babbles some more and nods.

When he opens the sliding door to the back deck, all eyes come to us, but my attention is drawn to Maverick and Tanner and the smirks on their handsome faces. I narrow my eyes on the two of them as I step outside. Even if I don't know exactly what it is, I'm starting to get the feeling they're up to *something*.

"You look good with a baby in your arms, dear brother," Margret tells Blake, and I don't see the look he gives her, because his back is to me, but I do catch her laugh. Also, she is not wrong: Blake does look good holding a baby. Then again, he'd probably look good holding just about anything. If he ever hit hard times, he could put out a calendar of him holding random objects and make enough to cover his expenses and then some.

"Where is my niece?" he asks her, and she motions to the couch.

"She passed out about five minutes after we got outside. She had a long day with Grandma." She focuses on Sampson. "Are you feeling better now, buddy?" At her question, Sampson holds out his arms to her, and she takes him with ease as I take up residence in the chair Blake unfolds for me.

"Do you want a beer, Everly?" Maverick asks, and I shake my head.

"Thanks, but I'm driving, and since I haven't had a drink in the last two years, I'm sure I'd either start acting like an idiot or pass out—neither of which would be good."

"I can't imagine you acting like an idiot," Tanner says, taking a seat next to his wife and resting his hand palm down on her belly. The action that is both sweet and protective makes me a little envious that I didn't get that from Lex while I was carrying Sampson.

"Trust me. I'm not the classiest drunk person," I tell him, and he grins.

"I think you and I are going to be great friends," Margret says, and I turn to look at her and smile. "We should all plan to go out after Cybil pops the baby out."

"That's not happening." Blake shakes his head, and my nose scrunches.

"I second that," Tanner agrees. "You know I love you like a sister, Margret, but my wife is not going out drinking with you . . . ever."

"You know, last time I checked, I was a grown woman with a mind of her own." Cybil glares at her husband. "There will never be a time when you can tell me what I can and cannot do."

"I'm a little offended you guys think I would get these two sweet girls in trouble," Margret inserts, looking between Blake and Tanner, but Maverick is the one to respond.

"Before you got pregnant with Taylor, I had to pick you up more than once, and I regretted answering my cell every time you called."

"I wasn't that bad," Margret grumbles, passing Sampson to Cybil when she reaches for him.

"You ran away from me and acted like I was trying to kidnap you."

"That only happened once, and I apologized the next day as soon as I woke up."

"And the time you decided we were going to play hide-and-seek, only I had no idea I was playing a game and was meant to find you?"

"I'm a mom now." She rolls her eyes. "I've obviously matured since then."

"Obviously," Blake mutters sarcastically, like he doesn't believe her.

"Whatever," she grouses, sounding as cranky as her brother, and I can't help but smile. "Anyway, are you guys going to cook dinner anytime soon? I'm starving."

"Yeah." Tanner gets up, kissing his wife on the side of the head before going over to start the grill.

"Do you need a break from all these girls, big guy?" Blake asks Sampson, and of course he goes right to him and smacks his jaw while babbling away.

"What's going on with you and my brother?" Margret asks me after the guys have taken up positions around the grill.

"I was wondering the same thing," Cybil says, and I shake my head at the two women who I just met and who obviously don't know about Blake's and my past encounters.

"Nothing is going on with us." I shift in my seat, feeling awkward under their scrutiny.

"Interesting." Margret taps her chin. "I can tell you're not lying, but there is some kinda vibe between the two of you."

"There aren't any vibes between us," I say, not completely sure what vibes she's talking about, and Cybil tips her head to the side.

"I heard about your first meeting with Blake. Tanner mentioned he was kind of a jerk."

"My brother, a jerk . . . ?" Margret gasps in fake shock, and Cybil turns to smile at her.

"I know it's hard to believe he would *ever* be rude." She turns back to me. "Once you get to know him, you'll find that he's actually really sweet."

"I wish I could say she's lying, but she's not. Blake might act like he doesn't care and come off rude sometimes—"

"Most of the time," Cybil cuts in.

"Okay, most of the time," Margret agrees. "But it's just his way."

"I'm sure he's a very nice guy," I reply. "That said, he's my boss, and I'm not even a little interested in him." *Gah, why does that feel like a lie?* "I just got out of a relationship with Sampson's father, and I'm not looking to get involved with anyone."

"I totally get that," Margret says quietly as she looks over to the couch, where her daughter's still sleeping. "I just ended things with Taylor's dad not long ago, and I know I'm not ready to get involved with anyone else for a long, long time."

"I'm sorry," I say as Cybil reaches out to take her hand.

"It's okay. It's for the best. Now, the only thing that matters is that he's still around for his daughter. I'm sure you get that having Sampson," she says, and I struggle with what to say, because the truth is, I doubt there will be a time when Lex is in Sampson's life.

Since I've been home, we still haven't spoken, and there's no way I'm going to force him to step up to the plate by taking him to court.

At the end of the day, I know he didn't want to be a dad, and there's no way I want to put my son in a position to be constantly let down by the guy who helped make him.

Thankfully, before I'm forced to say something, Sampson's cheery shriek fills the air, taking the attention off me.

"I think he might be hungry." Blake walks toward me with Sampson, and my heart does a strange thump inside my chest. "He was trying to get me to give him a banana, but I stood strong, not knowing if he should have one."

"He loves bananas," I reply, and he smiles. *Lord, what the hell is going on with me?* "Umm." I hold out my hands for Sampson to come to me, but he latches onto Blake even tighter. "I brought him his food. It's in his diaper bag." I start to stand, and he shakes his head.

"I can get it," he tells me, kissing the top of Sampson's head and making my stupid heart melt. "Is his bag in the living room?"

"Yeah," I practically whimper, and he nods before turning and walking away.

"Okay, I know I'm very pregnant, but I swear my ovaries just exploded," Cybil says, and I bite my lip so I don't blurt out my agreement.

"Eww," Margret mumbles. Then she asks, "You okay, Everly?"

"Great," I lie, because the truth is, I have no idea what the hell it is I'm feeling right now.

Chapter 5

EVERLY

I pull up in front of Live Life Adventures Lodge and put my car in park before grabbing my cell phone to check my messages. Yesterday, Cybil went into labor early and ended up having an emergency C-section. I was in the office when everything happened, but apparently Blake and Tanner rushed her to the hospital, where she eventually brought a very cute—judging by the photos—baby girl into the world.

Thankfully, both baby and mama are doing great, but with Tanner obviously out with his wife and newborn for the foreseeable future, things here at the lodge will be left up to Blake, Maverick, and me. I know we've been working toward this happening, but I thought I would have more time to settle in before stuff got real.

After typing a quick text to Maverick, letting him know I'm heading into the office and not to worry about things, I start to open my door but stop when my cell rings in my hand. The name and number combo on the screen is one I know all too well, and with my stomach in knots, I watch my phone continue to ring.

I know I should answer. I know I should, but the idea of speaking to my ex is not even a little appealing. Part of me is panicked that he's going to say he's changed his mind about having a relationship with his son; another part of me is worried I'll hate him even more if that's not why he's calling. After a deep breath, I slide my shaking finger across the screen and put the call on speaker.

"Lex." I go for casual, praying he doesn't hear the shake to my voice.

"Umm, hey, Everly." He clears his throat, and I wonder why he sounds so nervous. "How have you been?"

Really? I haven't spoken to him in weeks, and that's his question? How does he think I've been? "What's going on?"

"Well . . ." He clears his throat again. "I . . . well, I talked to my mom yesterday, and I . . ." He lets out a long sigh. "I told her about Sampson," he says, and I frown. The last he told me, he did not have much of a relationship with his parents, and I got that, because the way he described them made it seem like they would be the last people you would want in your life. "She wants to meet him."

"You're kidding, right?" I ask as anger curls up in the pit of my stomach.

"She's his grandmother," he replies, and red fills my vision as I stare at the lodge in front of me.

"I can't do this right now," I whisper, wondering if I might be having a heart attack. It feels like my heart is beating way too hard and that I might just puke at any moment.

"She doesn't live far from where you are now. You could just take him to meet her at a restaurant or something."

Oh my God, so he wants me to take my son to meet her on my own? He doesn't even want to be there when our son meets his grandmother for the first time?

"I just got to work. I'll text you later," I say in a rush, needing to get off the phone before I start to scream and say something I might regret. I knew he didn't care for our son, but for him to put me in this situation just shows me how little he ever cared about *me*.

"Everly, it's not a big deal."

Not a big deal?

"Stop," I hiss. "Just stop. I need to think about this," I say right before I hang up on him. When I get out of my car, my legs feel like Jell-O, and I'm seriously questioning my ability to make it across the distance between me and the steps to the deck, up them, and into the lodge without passing out.

"Everly," a deep voice calls, and before I can turn my head to confirm it's Blake, he's standing next to me with his concern-filled eyes roaming over my face. "What happened? Are you okay?"

"No." I shake my head, then—because he's there, looking tall, strong, and able—I fall into his arms, which don't hesitate to wrap around me. I burrow my face against his chest and dig my fingers into his tee as I start to cry. All the stress, sadness, anger, and hurt causes the tears I've been holding back ever since I found out I was pregnant to soak his shirt.

Without a word, he rubs my back; then I'm up in his arms and being carried like a child up the stairs and into the lodge. In the back of my mind, a voice is screaming at me, telling me that I should pull away and tell him that I'm okay, that I'm a big girl who can handle her own problems. But there's something about him that feels good, solid . . . safe.

When he takes a seat and adjusts me across his lap, he palms the side of my head, holding me firmly in place as I sob. I don't know how long we sit there like that, and I don't know what he says to me as I cry, even though I can hear his chest rumble against my ear. When the tears finally start to subside, my muscles bunch as I realize what an idiot I've been in front of him and that now I'm going to have to explain why I had a meltdown—at work, of all places.

"My dad has cancer." His words cut through the embarrassment and silence that have settled between us, and my heart hurts for a different reason. "He doesn't want anyone to know." His thumb, wrapped around the side of my neck, rubs up and down in a soothing motion, like I'm the one who still needs comfort. "It's been almost a year; he's in treatment now." Pain slices through my chest, and I squeeze my eyes closed and press closer to him, even though I doubt we could get any closer than we are right now.

"Lying to my mom and sister is killing me, but he doesn't want to worry them."

"Blake," I whisper, knowing that saying sorry will never be enough, and his warm breath touches the top of my head as his arms, still holding me, grow tighter.

"Sucks. I love my dad. I love my family."

"I know," I whisper, because even having never met his father, I have gotten to see him with both his mom and his sister, and I can tell how much he loves them.

"Please don't tell anyone about what I just told you."

"Never." I pull back just enough to look him in the eye, and his brow furrows. I'm sure I look a mess, but given what he's just said, my appearance doesn't really matter at the moment. "I do hate that you're keeping that secret." My fingers twitch in my lap with the urge to reach up and smooth the lines between his brows. "I understand why you're doing it, but it's also not fair to put you in that position." When he doesn't say anything, I shift uncomfortably, which reminds me that I'm still sitting on his lap. "Sorry." I move and take a seat next to him, adjusting my sweater, then swipe my palms down the front of my jeans. "I didn't mean to cry all over you." I wipe under my eyes, doubting my nonwaterproof mascara has stayed in place.

"You wanna tell me what happened?"

I bite my lip and quickly glance at him over my shoulder.

"You don't have to."

"I know," I say quietly as my hands twist in my lap. "My ex called me this morning." I take a breath, needing a moment to get my thoughts in order, a moment to try to figure out how to explain things. "He didn't want to be a dad, and since I wanted to be a mom, things didn't work out." I glance at him once more when he doesn't say anything. His expression gives nothing away, and I don't know if that makes me feel more relaxed or more on edge. "When I told him I was leaving, he was okay to see me go, and I hadn't spoken to him since, before today."

"You hadn't talked to him since you've been here?" he asks, sounding disgusted and irritated on my behalf.

"No. Like I said, he didn't want to be a father."

"Right," he grumbles, and I fight back a smile.

"Anyway." I pull in a deep breath and let it out slowly. "Today, he called to tell me that he told his mom about Sampson, and she wants to meet him."

"She wants to meet him?" I turn to face him at the repeat of my statement and notice his jaw is clenched. "What did you say?"

"I hung up on him, then proceeded to have a meltdown," I admit, and he reaches for my hand, which I give to him willingly.

"You don't want her to meet him?"

"I don't know." I study his fingers, which are about twice as big as mine. "He told me he didn't have a very good relationship with either of his parents, and the way he described them and his childhood didn't make it seem like his parents would be people you'd want to know or have around your child."

"Has your ex been involved at all?" he asks, and I shake my head, unwilling to tell him exactly how uninvolved he's been. When Sampson was born, he didn't sign his birth certificate, and when we came home from the hospital, he pretty much left us to do our own thing. He was either working or out with friends, and when he was around, he pretended like Sampson didn't exist and that I was a roommate just staying in his house. "You should tell him to fuck off."

"I know." And I do know I should tell him to take his wants and shove them where the sun doesn't shine. But there is a part of me that understands how important family is, and even though Lex isn't involved in Sampson's life, his parents could fill a little of that void—maybe not right now, but in the future—for him.

"I can see you're not going to do that, so I think you need to figure out for yourself how much you're willing to give and what you're willing to do. It's one thing to want your ex to have a relationship with your son, but it's another thing to tie yourself up in knots for his parents."

"You're right," I agree, because he *is* right. "It's just . . . I mean, how do I even know my ex wasn't lying about his parents? For all I know, they could be the nicest people."

"They could be." His fingers squeeze mine. "You won't know unless you meet with them." My spine stiffens at the idea. "If you want, I could go with you when that happens. You can feel them out and see if you'd be willing to let them meet Sampson." He turns his hand so his fingers lace with mine. "No matter what happens, you just need to remember you are in control; nothing can happen without your consent."

"Thank you." I lock my eyes with his, wanting him to see how much the last few minutes have meant to me. It's one thing to share these kinds of things with my mom, who is beyond partial, and another to have them with an outside person who is not at all involved and has nothing to gain.

"Anytime." His eyes drop to our hands that are still interlocked, and I wonder what he's thinking. He's not someone who can be easily read. His emotions are not visible through his expressions or mannerisms. He's a mystery, and even though I shouldn't want to solve the puzzle that is Blake, I still have the desire to find all the flat-edged pieces that belong to him so I can fit him together.

"We should get to work," I say after a moment, and he lifts his head, his eyes meeting mine.

With a jerk of his chin, he stands, pulling me up with him, then untangles our fingers, letting me go. I shouldn't feel alone, but I do. "Let me know if you need anything."

"Sure." I hold my breath and watch as he turns and walks away. It's not the first time I've felt confused when he's left my presence, but it is the first time I've felt as if I should have said something or done something to make him stay.

When he disappears out of sight, I look around the empty space surrounding me for a clue, from the gorgeous view of the tree-lined vista out the twenty-foot windows, to the interior of the lodge, and neither is able to tell me whether it's me or him who is running now.

Chapter 6

EVERLY

.

"Good, you're here," Blake says, stepping into the office, and it takes a lot of willpower to keep focused on the computer and to not pick up the stapler sitting a couple of inches away and toss it at his big head.

You would think that, after the moment we shared a couple of days ago, things between us would be different, but since then, he's gone back to avoiding me, which is beyond annoying at this point. And I know he's avoiding me. He's left the kitchen the moment I walked in, turned around and gone the opposite direction when he's seen me coming, and sent my calls to voice mail more than once.

"Are you ignoring me?" he asks. I hear the chair across from me creak under his weight as he takes a seat.

"I'm working. What do you need?" I keep my focus on the computer, wanting to make sure I don't mess up the food order that Janet emailed to me this morning.

"Will you look at me?"

"I don't need to look at you for you to tell me what you need."

"You're pissed." The surprise in his tone sets my teeth on edge. "Why are you pissed at me?"

That's a good question. I shouldn't be so angry with him, but the truth is, I feel disappointed and frustrated with him . . . and myself. I thought that after our conversation, things between us would change. I thought that him opening up to me and me opening up to him meant things between us had taken a turn for the better, but he showed me that I was wrong and proved I'm not a good judge of character.

"I know it might be hard to believe, but the world doesn't revolve around you, Blake."

"I don't know, Everly, but I'd bet my last dollar that if Mav was the one sitting across from you, you'd be all smiles, giggles, and sweetness."

With a different kind of anger now dancing hot through my veins, I turn and lock my gaze on his. "What is that supposed to mean?"

"Your crush on him is obvious," he says without breaking eye contact.

"Really?"

"Really." He leans in, and I don't know if I should laugh or scream in his face.

"What's going on here?" We both look at Maverick as he steps into the room, and I wave a hand out in Blake's direction.

"Your idiot friend here thinks I have a crush on you."

"Does he?" He raises a brow while crossing his arms over his chest.

"I've seen the two of you together," Blake rumbles, sounding irritated.

"Have you?" Maverick asks, sounding more curious than annoyed. "Together how? Because I can tell you that she's never sat on my lap at any point since knowing her."

My stomach bottoms out, and my cheeks burn with embarrassment. The only reason he'd say that is if he saw Blake and me together.

He turns, locking his eyes with mine. "I just came to see if Blake talked to you about learning to drive the four-wheelers, since we might need your help running supplies with the next group coming in."

"I haven't had a chance to talk to her about it yet," Blake tells him, and Maverick looks between the two of us, then scrubs his hands down his face.

"With Tanner out, the three of us are going to have to work together. I know we all thought we'd have more time to prepare, but we don't, so we need to put everything else on the back burner and focus on work."

"I've always been focused on work," I chime in, ignoring the strange energy pinging between the two men in the room. "And I've never driven a four-wheeler before, so a lesson probably wouldn't hurt."

"Blake will help you out with that," Maverick replies, looking at his friend. "Right?"

"I'll pick up one of the four-wheelers from Tanner's this evening, and tomorrow morning, we can drive up to one of the campsites we use."

"That's fine," I lie, because the idea of spending time alone with him is not even a little appealing.

"Great. I'll pick you up at your house at nine, if that works for you?"

"See you then." I glare at the door when he disappears, then mutter, "I know he's your friend, but if he ends up missing after tomorrow, I hope you will at least pretend you don't know what happened to him." I look up at Maverick. "I mean, not forever. I just need enough time to pack up my son and make it to Mexico." I shake my head when he laughs. "I'm serious."

"I know. That's why I'm laughing."

"I'm happy you find my annoyance comical."

"There is a lot I'm finding comical right now." He doesn't say more, and my eyes narrow on his.

"What does that mean?"

"Nothing." He glances at the clock on the wall. "I'm going to be away from the lodge for a couple of hours. I gotta run over to help Tanner set up the crib for Claire, since she should be getting released from the hospital in the next couple of days."

"That's so exciting." I can't help the smile that replaces my frown. "How's baby and mama doing?"

"Good but ready to be home." He tucks his hands into the front of his jeans. "You should give Cybil a call. I'm sure she'd be happy to hear from you."

"I will. I just didn't want to overwhelm her. I remember how stressful those first few days can be. When she gets home with Claire, I'll ask when I can stop by for a visit."

"She'd like that," he says, then checks the clock once more before lifting his chin and heading for the door. "I'll have my cell on. Just call if you need anything."

"I should be good," I assure him, and with a quiet goodbye, he takes off.

Just as I'm getting back into work, my cell vibrates, so I check to make sure it's not my mom. Instead, I find a message from Lex, asking if I've thought more about when I can take Sampson to meet his mother. With a knot in the pit of my stomach, I message him back that I'm still thinking about it. When I talked to my parents about his mother's request, neither of them seemed exactly thrilled about the idea. But they did say that if the shoe was on the other foot, they would hope to at least get the chance to meet their grandchild, and I can understand that.

The logical side of me knows I shouldn't hold Lex's parents responsible for him not wanting to be a part of Sampson's life, but the illogical side of me wants nothing to do with anything having to do with him, including his family. A minute after I send the text, he texts back one letter—K—and I can do nothing but roll my eyes.

After turning my phone facedown on the desk, I get back to work. I can only deal with one issue at a time, and right now, I need to work, not stress about my ex or the fact that I'm going to have to spend time alone with Blake.

Dressed in jeans, one of my college sweatshirts, and my sneakers, I tie my hair up into a ponytail, then look at my reflection and the bags under my eyes that are screaming for concealer. Last night, Sampson slept great. I, on the other hand, tossed and turned, overthinking the phone call I'd had with Lex before I went to bed. I told him that after thinking about it the last few days, I would meet his mom and dad at noon on Saturday for lunch at the Root, and he let me know that he would unsurprisingly not be there.

He also let me know that his new girlfriend would be moving in with him soon, so after meeting his parents, I shouldn't text him but instead use his mom as a go-between. Of course I asked, "A go-between for what?" since he made it clear he doesn't want a relationship with Sampson, and he told me not to be "dramatic." I then proceeded to lose my mind before hanging up on him. How I could be so wrong about someone is anyone's guess, but one thing is for sure—I'm not a good judge of character, and men suck.

With a sigh, I poke my head into Sampson's room. I make sure he's okay, then end up adding foundation, blush, and mascara and filling in my brows before getting Sampson dressed for the day. I walk down the stairs with him on my hip, and my brows drag together when I hear my mom and a man both laughing from the direction of the kitchen.

Curious who's here, I head around the corner, and my heart drops into the pit of my stomach when I see Blake sitting at the island with my mom, the two of them drinking coffee and smiling. Lord, I don't think I've ever seen Blake really smile, and that's probably a good thing based on the way my stomach feels, seeing it now.

"Da, da, da!" Sampson screeches, causing me to jump and Blake and Mom to turn my way. Blake's eyes lock with mine for a moment, something in them making me feel warm. "Da, da, da, da!" he yells louder as he thrusts his body forward to get down.

"That's Blake, baby," I tell him gently as I place him on his feet, and he starts screaming, "Blay, Blay!" as he runs across the room and right to Blake. I let out a long sigh as I watch Blake bend to pick him up and hold him over his head, grinning and looking like a magazine ad. Seriously, it's annoying that I can still find him attractive. Then again, I'm guessing most women would find him handsome, with his blondish hair, scruffy jaw, and lumberjack look he's got going on today, including a red-and-black flannel with a vest over it.

"Hey, big guy," he says, and Sampson's laughter rings through the room. Dragging my eyes off them, I look over at my mom and roll my eyes at the look of awe on her face, and she turns my way, quickly clearing the expression.

"Hey, honey, you look cute." She pushes up off the stool she's on, and I rub my hands down the front of my jeans. "Do you want some coffee?"

"I can get it." I walk past Blake and Sampson, who are now carrying on a conversation, and grab a to-go mug from the cupboard. As I'm filling my cup, Blake places Sampson on his feet, then lets him lead him across the space to the living room where his toys are, and Mom comes over to stand next to me.

"Sorry," she whispers. "I should have sent you a text or something to let you know he was here already."

"It's fine," I whisper back, and her hand gently brushes a stray tress off my forehead.

"Are you sure?"

Hearing the concern in her voice, I meet her gaze. "Yeah." I plaster a smile on my face, and her shoulders relax.

"Sampson seems to really like him?" The statement sounds almost like a question.

"He does." I take a sip of my coffee while glancing into the living room, where Blake is now sitting on the floor with Sampson, playing blocks with him. "He acted the same way when we were at Tanner's for dinner. Wherever Blake went, he wanted to go."

"It's sweet that he's so good with him." She shakes her head and carries on. "I expected him to be grumpy, or quiet, but he was charming from the moment I opened the door."

Blake, charming? Sweet, I can see, but charming? Not so much.

"I like his energy."

"You like his energy?" I repeat, and she nods. "Are you the Dalai Lama now?" I ask, and she starts to laugh, then looks at the clock. I know what's coming, because it's almost nine, and since I can remember, she's done the same thing every weekday morning.

"It's almost time for Sam and me to watch *Joe's Morning Joe*."

"Right." I kiss her cheek, then set down my coffee and go to the living room, where I pick up my boy and look at Blake. "Are you ready?" He lifts his chin, then gets up off the floor while I smother my sweet boy's face with kisses that make him giggle. "Be good for Grandma while I'm gone," I tell him, and he gurgles something before going into my mom's open arms. "I'll have my phone on me if you need anything."

"We'll be fine, won't we?" she asks Sampson as he attempts to eat her shirt, then looks at me. "Don't forget your dad and I are leaving for Idaho tonight when you get home."

Damn, how could I forget they're going to see my brother and his family for the weekend? Now I'm even more anxious about seeing Lex's parents tomorrow, because I will have to do it alone. And no way am I going to tell my mom, because I know she's been looking forward to spending time with my nieces, and I don't want her to cancel the trip.

"I haven't forgotten," I say as I go to the kitchen to grab Sampson a frozen chewy out of the freezer and my coffee off the counter. Giving him the toy, I kiss his cheek, then grab my purse and vest while Blake says goodbye. When we get outside and I see his oversize truck parked at the curb with a trailer attached to it carrying a dirty black four-wheeler, I bite my lip. It's one thing to think about having to spend time alone with him . . . but another thing to know I'm going to be spending the *next few hours* alone with him.

"Let me help you with that." He opens the passenger door for me, and I use the foot rail to heft myself up into the seat as his hand rests against my back, searing through my shirt and imprinting on my skin.

"Thanks," I mumble, tucking my feet inside the truck.

"Buckle up." He slams the door, and I jerk the seat belt across me as he jogs around the hood of the truck. When he gets in behind the wheel, I remind myself this is not a date and I have no reason to be nervous. "Ready?"

"Yep," I say, and as he turns on the engine, the sound of quiet hip-hop fills the cab.

"Your mom seems nice." He lifts his hand to wave past me, and I turn to find my mom and Sampson both waving from the open front door.

"She's the best." I wave at her and my son, then tuck my hands between my legs as the truck pulls away from the curb. "How's your dad doing?" When he doesn't answer right away, I doubt he's going to, but then he lets out a long breath and starts to tap the steering wheel.

"He only tells me as much as he has to. He knows I'll bring up him telling my mom and sister if he says he's not okay."

"Oh," I say quietly, squeezing my legs together tightly to hold my hands in place and not reach over and touch him. "You're the only person he's told, the only one who knows?"

"Yeah." He takes a hand off the steering wheel to run his fingers through his hair. "The day I met you at your dad's office, I was planning on telling my grandmother, but she wasn't there, so I took it as a sign that maybe she shouldn't know."

"I bet she would want to know," I tell him honestly. I mean, I know for sure his mom and sister would want to know as well, but as a mom, I would want to know that my baby was sick, and I don't think that changes no matter your kid's age.

"I don't know. She's not exactly been acting like herself since she got a boyfriend who's half her age."

"The guy she's dating is half her age?" I ask, and he glances over at me.

"Maybe not half, but he's forty-five tops, so a lot younger than her."

"Go, Grandma." I smile when I notice his jaw twitch. "Let me guess—you don't like him. I can't say that's shocking."

"What does that mean?"

"You don't seem to like much of anything or anyone," I say, pointing out the obvious.

"I like plenty of things, and people. I just got shit on my mind."

"I know, and believe me—I have sympathy for you and what you're having to deal with, but honestly, you're like a big bear with a splinter in its paw, and instead of letting anyone help you, you're growling and slashing at everyone around you."

"Did you just compare me to a cranky bear?"

"I did, and I won't take it back." I focus my attention out the window. "You're not the only person dealing with shit that sucks," I mumble, and not surprisingly, he doesn't reply.

The rest of the drive is as awkward as one would expect it to be, so I'm more than a little thankful when we get to the parking area at the base of one of the mountains and I am able to escape the confines of the cab. As he unloads the four-wheeler from the trailer, I sit on the tailgate of the truck and tip my head back to the sun, closing my eyes.

"What are you thinking about?"

His question pulls me out of my thoughts, and I open one eye and find him standing about a foot away with one of the trailer ties in his hand and a baseball cap on his head that looks way too good on him.

"Absolutely nothing, just enjoying the sun for a minute. Do you need my help?"

"No, just gonna back it down—then we can take off," he says, so I sit up and watch him reverse the four-wheeler off the trailer; then I hop down off the tailgate when he's done and help him slide the lift back in place. "Thanks." He looks from the four-wheeler to me with an odd expression.

"What?"

"Nothing, let's do this." He goes to the machine, gets on, and motions for me to come closer. I listen to him as he gives me a rundown of the gas, brakes, and how to use them, and honestly, it all seems easy enough. "Do you think you got it?"

"I think so," I say, and he jumps off and pats the seat.

"Sit here." With a shrug, I straddle the seat and grab the handles. "Now, I just want you to get a feel for the gas. Pull back nice and slow."

"Okay." I pull back on the gas, and I must do it a little too hard, because I end up kicking up dirt as I shoot forward, barely missing Blake when he jumps out of the way.

"Use the brakes!" he starts yelling, and I do—only I do it too hard and almost end up over the handlebars as I skid to a stop. I hold my hand against my chest over my pounding heart and start to turn to tell him that I don't think I'm cut out for driving when I'm dragged off the seat and wrapped in a tight hug. "Are you okay? Shit, I knew I shouldn't have let you ride alone."

"I think I might need another lesson," I tell him quietly, trying not to think about how good it feels to be in his arms, and he pulls back enough to look at me, then drops his head back on his shoulders and lets out a long sigh.

"Sorry, babe, but you're not getting back on that thing alone."

"At least I know what *not* to do now," I tell him when he lets me go.

"Yeah, at least." He throws one leg over the seat, then grabs my hand. "Climb on." I look from his face to the small space in front of him, and my heart starts pounding for a different reason. "Come on," he orders, giving my hand a tug, and I carefully put myself in front of him and hold my breath as I sit between his spread thighs. When his hands grab mine, placing them on the handles, and he covers them with his own, his breath brushes against my ear. "Breathe, Everly."

"Breathe. Right." Breathing would probably be smart. I mean, I do kind of need oxygen to survive. It's just that it's one thing to be stuck in the cab of the truck with him, but it's a completely different thing to be surrounded by his warmth, strength, and scent. Unsurprisingly, my body reacts to his nearness and warm breath against my ear as he explains what we're going to do. When he uses my hand to pull back on the gas and we start to drive forward, my nipples pebble and the space between my legs tingles.

Driving a four-wheeler should not feel like foreplay, but as we begin to drive faster and head up the hill into the woods, my breath speeds up.

"You doing okay?" he asks over the engine, and I can only nod, sure he'd know by the sound of my voice how turned on I am, which is as confusing as it is inappropriate. I should not be interested in someone who aggravates me as much as he does. "When we get up to the first turnaround, I'm going to let you take over controlling the gas and brakes."

"I don't think that's smart," I inform him, and he laughs.

"You'll be fine. You've been in charge this whole time."

"Oh." I glance down at our hands and notice that his covering mine are relaxed, and I really am the one regulating how fast we're going.

"We're going to start slowing down so we can pull over up ahead," he says, and I bring us to a stop at a small clearing a couple of minutes later.

"You did good," he tells me, resting his hand on my hip as he gets off from behind me. "This is one of the spots guests stop at for lunch on the first day of their trip. Normally, we don't need to come up here, but there are some great views."

"It's so pretty. I've actually never been up here before."

"You haven't?" he asks as I step up next to him and look through the trees.

"I was never much of an outside-activities kind of girl growing up. I was too busy doing nerd-girl things, like lying in bed reading."

"I can't imagine you as a nerd." His gaze travels over my hair and face.

"I was." I shift on my feet and drop my eyes from his. "Or I still am. I just don't spend all my time reading anymore."

"Having a kid will do that."

"You're right about that," I say. "So where are we going now?"

"To the campsite we use."

"What will I be doing if I have to drive up here alone?" The idea is a little nerve racking to even think about.

"Just dropping off supplies for the day's activities or meals if needed. And we'll try our best to not let that happen. It's just going to be tricky on days when the canoes need to be dropped off or if we need to meet the guests with the bus."

"I don't mind helping however you need me to," I tell him. The last thing I want him, Maverick, or Tanner to think is that I'm not pulling my weight and then let me go.

"I know your son is a priority."

"He is, but my mom is totally okay with watching him. Believe me, I mentioned putting him in day care once, and she just about lost her mind."

"I bet she did. He's a sweet kid." He smiles, then turns toward me and reaches up to my face. I hold my breath as he slides his fingers through the hair at the side of my head. "Something's in your hair," he says quietly; then his eyes lock with mine, and I swear electricity fills the air between us as his hand curves around my ear. Lost in the contact, I drop my gaze to his mouth and lick my bottom lip, wondering what his mouth would feel like against mine. When I lift my eyes back up to his, I notice the sea-green color has darkened to match the forest around us as his fingers slide back into my hair. I automatically start to lean into him, then jump when a bird screeches nearby. How close we are standing and what I'm doing registers, and I take a step back, tucking my hands into the front pocket of my vest.

"Thanks." I clear my throat. "Well, should we go?" I don't wait for him to answer; I turn for the four-wheeler, reminding myself over and over to not let my hormones make me into an idiot and to focus on the job.

Chapter 7

EVERLY

Sitting on the top step of the lodge, I type a quick message to my mom to let her know that I should be home soon and that I'm just waiting for my cab. One thing I didn't think about when Blake said he was going to pick me up this morning was that I wouldn't have my car with me when work was done.

"I was looking for you," Blake says from behind me, and I look over my shoulder and watch him walk across the deck after locking the door. "Are you ready to leave?"

"Yeah, I finished up everything in the office. My ride should be here soon."

"What?" He frowns at me, and I frown back. Lord, with him around, I will need Botox before I know it.

"What do you mean *what*?"

"What ride?" His frown grows deeper.

"My cab."

"Why would you call a cab to come pick you up when I'm going to take you home?"

"I didn't know you were going to take me home. You never mentioned it," I say, pointing out the obvious.

"Why would I drive you to work, then leave you stranded?" he asks, sounding annoyed. "And if you hadn't been ignoring me all morning, you would have heard me tell you when we got back here that you should come find me when you were ready to go."

Did he? I don't remember that. Then again, I was working extra hard to block him out, which wasn't easy after whatever that was that happened between us.

"I wasn't ignoring you," I fib, and he gives me a look that states clearly that he knows I'm lying.

"Call the cab company and tell them you got a ride and don't need them," he orders, and I shake my head.

"That would be rude. I'm not going to do that when someone is already on their way up here."

"Fine." He takes a seat next to me on the step. "When they get here, I'll pay them, and we can take off."

"Don't be ridiculous." I roll my eyes. "I'll just take the cab home, and you can go about your evening."

"I'm taking you home, Everly," he states firmly, and I want to say something snarky but keep my mouth closed. He grunts, which makes it difficult to not smile. How I can find his crankiness cute is still a mystery to me.

When the cab arrives a few minutes later, I think about running and jumping into the back seat just to be difficult, but I doubt I would even make it, because he gets up before I can get my butt off the step I'm sitting on.

"You really didn't have to do this," I tell him as we walk to his truck after he pays the driver, who did not look upset in the least, but that could be because Blake gave him a whole bunch of cash, way more than the ride would have cost.

"It's not a big deal." He pulls the keys for his truck out of his pocket, then opens the door for me to get in with a quiet reminder to buckle up before he slams it closed.

As we pull out onto the main road, the silence between us feels heavy, and I wonder what he's thinking, but instead of asking, I focus my attention out the window.

"When are you meeting your ex's parents?" The out-of-the-blue question throws me, and I glance over at him. I don't know why I thought he forgot about me telling him that, but I did.

"Umm . . . tomorrow." I let my head fall back against the headrest. "Sampson and I are going to meet them for lunch at the Root."

"Alone?"

"Yeah, I would have taken my mom, but she and my dad are going to see my brother and his family in Idaho." I sigh, then add, "I wouldn't have planned it for then, but I forgot all about their trip until she reminded me this morning, and I don't want to have to message Lex to tell him that I have to reschedule."

"Why not?"

"A lot of reasons, but the main one being I never want to speak to him again."

"Got it," he mutters. "What time are you meeting them?"

"Noon," I say; then, when that same heavy silence begins to settle between us once more, I blurt out, "Are you doing anything this weekend?"

"Just catching up on work, taking care of stuff around my house."

"Okay, but what about fun stuff?"

"Fun stuff?" He glances over at me.

"You know, spending time with friends or doing something you love, baking, knitting, killing poor, defenseless animals," I prompt, and he laughs—*really* laughs—making me feel oddly powerful.

"I don't hunt, knit, or bake. Sunday, I'll have dinner with my parents, sister, and Taylor."

"Well, that's fun at least."

"Yeah," he agrees, shifting in his seat like he's uncomfortable. The rest of the drive is quiet, and when he pulls up in front of my parents' house a few minutes later, I'm equally anxious to get away from him and disappointed that I won't see him for a few days.

"Thanks again for the ride." I unhook my belt and am starting to reach for the handle when he calls my name. Pausing, I turn to look at him, then raise a brow when he doesn't say anything more. Instead, he just stares at me, looking like he's at war with himself. "Okay then, have a great weekend."

I push the door open and get out, then shut it behind me. As I head up the walkway, I wonder what it is he wanted to say. But I don't have long to ponder it, because the minute I get inside my parents' house, Sampson takes up all my attention, which is probably a good thing.

$\sim$

With nervous energy making me feel sick to my stomach, I pull into a parking spot just out front of the Root and wonder for the millionth time today if I should have just called Lex to cancel this meeting until sometime when I wouldn't have to face his parents alone. I know I'm a grown woman with a child, but I really wish that my mom were here to reassure me that everything is going to be okay.

With a quick glance at the clock, I see it's almost noon, and I take a deep breath, shut down the engine, and grab Sampson's diaper bag off the passenger seat. I tuck my cell phone and wallet into the front pocket, then get out. As I start to open the back door to remove Sampson from his car seat, I notice a man approaching wearing a baseball cap, a deep-green hoodie, jeans, and boots. It takes a second for my brain to catch up, and when it does, my heart starts to gallop inside my chest.

"What are you doing here?" The question is quiet, or it sounds quiet to me because of the blood currently pumping hard through my veins, the *woosh-woosh* sound of it so loud I can hear it in my ears.

Stopping just in front of me, Blake tucks his hands into the front pockets of his jeans. "I didn't want you or Sampson to be alone." He glances into the back seat. "I was going to ask if I could come with you but didn't think you'd say yes."

"So you just showed up," I say, and he shrugs. "Thank you." I swallow over the lump that has suddenly formed in my throat while my eyes start to water.

"Come here, Everly," he says gently, holding open his arms, and I don't hesitate to step into his embrace and wrap my arms around his waist. "It's going to be okay." His hold tightens as I nod. "And if it's not, I'll find a way to get you guys out of there, okay?"

"Yeah," I reply, and after a quick squeeze, he lets me go and steps back to open the rear door all the way.

The moment Sampson sees him, he starts to yell "Da, da, da, da!" while kicking his feet and reaching his arms out for Blake, and if I didn't know any better, I'd think he keeps referring to Blake as *Dad*.

"All right, big guy, you're free," he says once he's cleared the door of the car, and Sampson wraps his chubby little arms around Blake's neck and hugs him, making my heart melt. "Are you ready?" His eyes come to me, and I want to say no, but I also want to get this over with.

"Yep."

"Liar." He smiles, taking the diaper bag from me and placing it over his shoulder, then grabs my hand. My first instinct is to pull away, but the connection to him right now makes me feel safe and less anxious, so I relax. "Let's go eat some food."

"I don't think I'm going to be able to eat," I mumble when I see the couple waiting outside the entrance to the restaurant, watching us closely as we approach.

I didn't ask Lex what his parents looked like; then again, I guess I didn't need to. His dad looks like him. They both have the same tall, lanky build, dark hair with hints of silver, and olive skin. His mom is the opposite—petite and blonde—and not happy, judging by the scowl on her face. Jeff, like Lex, is a very handsome man, the silvering of his hair and the wrinkles forming around his eyes making him seem more interesting than old. Ginny, on the other hand, looks tired. Even with her wrinkle-free skin and her blonde hair that's blown out to perfection, I can see the stress around her eyes that cosmetics and facials can't hide.

"Ginny, Jeff?" I ask when we're close enough I don't have to raise my voice, and Jeff smiles, while Ginny's frown deepens as she glances between Sampson and Blake.

"Lex didn't mention you were bringing someone with you," Ginny says in greeting, and I notice then that Blake's hold on my hand is tighter than it was.

"Ginny." Jeff sighs, reaching out his hand before I can respond to his wife. "It's nice to meet you, Everly." I let go of Blake to take his hand. "And this must be Sampson."

"Yes, and my friend Blake," I say to introduce them, and he shakes Blake's hand, then reaches out to Sampson, who clings to Blake, resting his head against his chest and tucking his hand in his mouth.

"He's cute," he tells me.

"He looks nothing like Lex," Ginny inserts, and my stomach twists violently while Blake's entire body tightens next to mine. "He looks like your boyfriend's kid."

"Ginny!" Jeff snaps, and she turns to glare at her husband.

"It's true. Look at him." She waves her hand out to Blake and Sampson.

"I can assure you that he is Lex's son," I say in defense.

"I want a DNA test."

"Pardon." Blake's voice rumbles so deep that I feel it vibrate through my cells.

"Jesus, Ginny, what the fuck?" Jeff hisses.

"If he's Lex's boy, then a DNA test will prove it."

"That is not happening," I tell her, balling my hands into fists to keep from reaching out and slapping her. I've never in my life had the urge to cause someone harm until this moment, and it's honestly taking all my strength to keep myself in check.

"Why? Because you know he's not my son's kid?" she asks, and I take a step toward her without thinking, taking pleasure when her eyes widen.

"This meeting is done." Blake grabs hold of my arm as Jeff grabs Ginny's hand and starts to tug her away from us, ignoring the glare she sends his way.

"It was nice meeting you, Everly. And sorry about this," Jeff says over his shoulder while pulling his sputtering wife with him across the parking lot.

"Calm down, babe." Blake wraps his hand around the back of my neck, and I spin around to face him, then reach out for my boy. Once he's in my arms, I hold his head against my chest, just needing to feel his weight.

"Did that just happen?" I ask Blake when I meet his gaze, and his jaw twitches.

"Unfortunately," he responds as I kiss the top of Sampson's head, and Blake places his hand against my lower back and leads me toward the restaurant.

"I didn't think I could eat before; I really don't think I can eat now."

"Then you can watch me eat. I don't want you driving when you're shaking like you are," he says, and I start to tell him that I'm not shaking but realize he's right. My body is still vibrating from the adrenaline dumped into my system after that scene.

"Maybe sitting down for a few minutes would be smart," I agree as he opens the door for me to walk in ahead of him.

"Sit where you like." An older gentleman greets us with two menus, and Blake takes them before leading us to a half-circle booth in the back of the room that's away from everyone else. Once we're seated, Sampson crawls out of my arms and uses the back of the booth to walk to Blake, who grabs hold of him and settles him on his lap.

"Are you hungry, big guy?" Blake asks him, moving the silverware out of his reach when he tries to grab for it.

"I'm sure he is. He hasn't eaten lunch yet," I tell him, digging through his diaper bag for one of his rags so I can wipe the drool off his chin and a toy so that he has something to keep him occupied for a couple of minutes.

"They have mashed potatoes. Do you think he could eat that?" he asks me, taking the rag and wiping Sampson's face himself, then holding the small duck for him and squeezing it so it squeaks.

"Yeah, he also likes chicken if it's chopped up small." I glance at the menu, and the pepper-jack cheeseburger and fries combo actually makes my mouth water.

"Chicken and mashed potatoes it is." He pushes the menu away, and I shake my head.

"I can get something for Sampson and me to share. You should get what you want."

"That is what I want," he says, and even though I know he's lying, it's still sweet. "Are you going to eat something?"

"The pepper-jack burger looks good," I say, and he smiles softly, then turns his attention to the waitress, who comes over with a pad of paper and a pen, and I blink, recognizing her.

"Hey, big brother." Margret grins, then transfers that same smile to me. "Everly." Her gaze pings between the two of us. "Funny seeing you two here . . . together . . . on a Saturday for lunch."

"Margret." Blake sighs.

"Hey, little dude." She picks up Sampson when he reaches for her. "Are you feeling like a third wheel on this date?"

"Margret," Blake repeats, and she laughs, while my cheeks warm. I learned from Blake the other day that they're twins, and when she smiles you can definitely see the resemblance.

"Okay, okay." She waves him off. "What can I get you two?"

Quickly, Blake gives her our order, and I tell her what I would like to drink; then she passes Sampson back to Blake and tells us that she'll be back in a minute.

"I didn't know she works here."

"Yeah, she's helped out here most weekends since she was in high school."

"That's cool." I hold Sampson's hand as he walks around the booth to me. You'd think that with Blake, Margret, and me being so close in age, we would have known each other growing up. But I learned when we were all at dinner at Tanner and Cybil's place that their family actually lives a town over, so they went to one of our rival schools. Not that I was involved in anything that I would consider them rivals for; I didn't participate in sports or go to football games. I was a part of the book club, but we never competed with any other school to show our master reading powers.

"So do you feel up to talking about what happened with your ex's parents?" he asks quietly, and my nose scrunches. "If I'd known me being here would make his mom act like that, I wouldn't have come."

"I'm glad you came." I settle Sampson on my lap and give him his bottle when he reaches for where it's tucked in the side pocket of the diaper bag. "It's better to know that people are crazy up front."

"I guess that's one way to look at it," he says, studying me. "So what now?"

"Nothing, I'm done with them and with Lex. I don't need or want them in my life, and I for sure do *not* want them around my son."

"I get that, and I don't blame you."

"Also, they can't say I didn't try." I let out a breath and kiss the top of Sampson's head when he rests back against me.

"All right, here are your drinks," Margret announces, sliding a Sprite in front of me and a Coke across to Blake. "Your food should be ready soon." She plops down in the booth next to her brother and glances between us. "So what are you young 'uns up to today? Anything fun?" She nudges Blake in the side. "Stop frowning."

"After lunch, I was thinking about taking Sampson to the park near my parents' house," I cut in when he turns his frown on her.

"Are you going with her?" She looks at Blake, and his eyes meet mine.

"You can come if you want. Mostly, I just chase Sampson around."

"We could do that, or we could go to my friend's place. He and his wife own a farm not far from here, and they have a couple of alpacas, pigs, goats, and cows."

"Really?" I ask, and he shrugs.

"Look at you two, making plans." Margret sighs happily, resting her elbows on the table and her chin on the top of her hands. "And what about dinner? What are you guys doing for dinner?"

"Margret." He shakes his head, and she smiles at him, then me.

"Blake loves pizza, but not just any pizza. The buffalo pizza from Rosco's on Main. I think that's near your parents' house."

"Margret," he repeats, and she ignores him and continues.

"Tomorrow, you should come to dinner at our parents' house. My mom's making her killer meatloaf, and the kids could play together."

"You just don't know when to stop, do you?" He lets out an annoyed breath.

"Stop what?" she asks her brother while batting her lashes. "Everly and I are friends, and as a friend, I'm inviting her to our parents' house for dinner," she tells him, then gets up. "I need to go check on my tables. I'm hoping to leave this afternoon with enough money to pay my car payment this month."

When she bounces away, Blake glares at her back, and I press my lips together to keep from laughing. It's obvious that Margret is a force of nature, and when she gets something in her head, there is no stopping her.

"You don't have to come to my parents' for dinner." He clears his throat. "Unless you want to come; then you're more than welcome. My mom would be happy to have you and Sampson around."

"I wouldn't want to make you uncomfortable," I tell him, watching his brow furrow as I take the bottle from Sampson and rub his back.

"Plus, my parents are going to be coming home tomorrow, so I should probably try to get some stuff done around the house."

"You're not going to make me uncomfortable," he says, and it would be easier to believe him if he wasn't still frowning. "You should join us."

"I'll think about it," I reply softly, and he lifts his chin slightly, then reaches for Sampson to help him across to sit on his lap once more.

"And I'm serious about going to my friend's farm after lunch, if you wanna do that."

"I would like that," I say, and he seems to visibly relax.

A moment later, our lunch arrives, and he and I take turns feeding Sampson bites of food from a small plate Margret brings over. When we're done, he pays the tab, even though I try.

When we leave the Root, we decide it will be easier to leave his truck behind, so we take my car to his friend's property, which happens to be in the middle of a valley with views of the mountains and blue skies as far as the eye can see. As we arrive, we find Sampson asleep, so instead of going to explore the farm, we pull a blanket from my trunk—one I forgot when moving—and take it to a field of yellow and white wildflowers.

Then, with Sampson napping, the sun shining, I spend the afternoon with Blake. And Lord help me, but I know I'm screwed, because I totally have a crush on my complicated, frustrating, and absolutely endearing boss.

Chapter 8

BLAKE

With the sound of kids laughing and parents chatting around me, I stand with my arms crossed over my chest on the edge of the little kids' play area at the park, my eyes on Sampson. When he woke up from his nap while we were still at the farm, we took him to see the cows, but we found out quickly that he wanted nothing more than to run, so Everly suggested that we move to the park, where it would be safer for him. With him being so little and still so unstable on his feet, it's difficult not to hover even now, especially with other kids who don't seem to understand the definition of personal space.

I start to step forward to go to him when a little boy, probably four or five years old, zooms past him, causing him to wobble and fall on his bottom. But when he doesn't cry and just gets back up, I relax . . . only to brace when the same kid runs past him again, this time purposely bumping into him.

"Hey, be careful!" I bark, and the kid looks at me with wide eyes before running off, yelling for his mom.

"You know, it's not really appropriate to glare or yell at other people's kids," Everly says quietly, and I glance down at her. "It also looks like you're no longer the hot guy at the park but enemy number one." She jerks her chin out slightly, and I follow the movement, noticing that the mom the little boy ran to is currently glaring at me. "If she comes over to beat you up, you're on your own."

"That kid was a dick."

"You're also not allowed to call other people's kids *dicks*, even if they are dicks." She grins.

"I'll try to remember that." I watch her laugh, and my fingers twitch with the urge to tangle in her hair so I can tilt her head back and kiss her pretty mouth.

"Da, da, da, da!" We both turn to Sampson when he starts to yell. Since he can't actually form words and has no real understanding of what he's saying, I shouldn't feel so fucking smug knowing he's calling out to me, but I do.

"What's up, big guy?" I walk over to where he's standing, and he holds out his arms for me to pick him up; then he points to the swings.

"Only one more time," Everly tells him, pulling his hoodie up over his head, and I notice the slight chill that's beginning to fill the evening air. "Then we need to go home to eat dinner, and you have to have a bath before bed."

"No." He shakes his head and pats my cheek, babbling something with "mama and da" mixed in.

"Sorry, big guy. Your mom's the boss," I tell him, and he shakes his head again and babbles some more as we walk to where the swing set is at the opposite end of the park. Once I have him in one of the baby seats, I push him, listening to him giggle as Everly makes faces at him while she takes dozens of pictures with her phone.

Watching her with her son makes my chest feel tight. She's beautiful, really fucking beautiful, inside and out. Over the last week, I've come to the realization that fighting the pull I feel toward her is pointless. She's woken up something inside me I didn't know was asleep, emotions I forgot I even had—happiness, protectiveness, jealousy, excitement. Until her, I didn't realize how much I had closed down, and I'm not sure why I did, but she makes me want to do better, be better. Being with her and Sampson centers me more than it scares me.

"Did you hear me?"

I come out of my thoughts on that question and find Everly watching me closely.

"Sorry, no. What did you say?"

"I asked if you wanted to join us for dinner?" Her cheeks are tinged with pink that I'm not sure is from the cold. "I mean, you don't have to if you have plans or a date or something."

"No date." I hold her eye. "Dinner sounds good," I answer instantly, the list of things I needed to get done today seeming less important than it did this morning.

"Okay, good." She licks her lips and clears her throat before stopping the swing. "Time to go, baby." Sampson's bottom lip wobbles, and tears fill his eyes as she lifts him out of the seat. "Oh, don't do that." She kisses his cheek once she has him settled on her hip, and he starts to cry harder as we walk to the parking lot.

"You're killing me, big guy." I hold out my hands for him to come to me, then toss him in the air and fly him around until his tears dry up and he starts to laugh.

"Sucker." Everly shakes her head when we reach her car, and I don't even try to deny I'm obviously weaker than her when it comes to his tears.

"Start the engine and turn on the heat. I'll get him buckled in," I tell her when she reaches for him, and he clings to me.

"Thanks," she says softly, opening the door.

As she slides in behind the wheel, I get Sampson into his seat and strapped in. "See you in a few minutes." I kiss Sampson's hand when he places it against my mouth, then get out and slam the door.

"I'll meet you at the house," she tells me when she gets the window rolled down. "We can just call and order from somewhere once I get Sam settled, if that works for you."

"I'm good with that," I assure her, and with a nod, she rolls the window back up, then waits for me to get into my truck, which I'd picked up from the Root so that I could follow her to the park.

When we arrive at her parents' place a few minutes later, I park right behind her, then help her get Sampson and his diaper bag inside, a task that is more difficult than one would think it would be. How she's been doing all this on her own for almost a year is mind-blowing to me, and it just shows how strong women are when they don't have any other choice.

"Do you know what you want to eat?" she asks as she walks through the small entryway in the front of the house. She turns on lights as she goes to the living room, across from the kitchen, where she places Sampson near his toys.

"I'm good with whatever."

"Pizza?" she asks, glancing at me quickly before turning on the TV and putting it on some kids' show with brightly colored singing animals. "Your sister mentioned you like a pizza from Rosco's."

"I do, but if you're not in the mood for that, I'm good with whatever you want," I tell her, and she rolls her eyes as she walks toward me.

"I'm going to make Sam some noodles and peas for dinner. Do you want a plate of that?" She raises a brow, and I must make a face, because she laughs. "I thought so." She passes me. "I'll call in the order for Rosco's once I get Sam something to eat."

"I can put in an order for us." I pull out my cell from my back pocket. "Do you know what you want?"

"They have an antipasto salad there that's good. Can I get that with grilled chicken and balsamic vinaigrette?" She pulls out a plastic container from the fridge as I dial the number and put my phone to my ear. "Oh, also an order of cheesy breadsticks and a slice of chocolate cake?"

"Is that all?" I raise a brow, listening to the phone ring.

"Buffalo wings also sound good." My eyes travel over her from her face to her now bare feet. Even with her abundance of curves, she's still tiny, so I have no idea where she's going to put all that food. "Don't look at me like you're judging me."

"I'm not judging you."

"Good, because it would suck if I had to kick your ass after the great day we've had," she tells me, and I fight back a smile as a guy named Mark answers the phone and asks for my order. Once I give it to him, along with the number for my credit card and her address, I hang up and tuck my cell back into my pocket.

"They said it's going to be an hour or a little longer before our food will get here."

"That works. It should give me enough time to get Sam fed, bathed, and maybe even in bed." She dumps a handful of frozen peas in a strainer, along with the pasta from the fridge, then runs hot water over them.

"What can I help with?" I start to step farther into the kitchen but stop when I feel a tug on the leg of my jeans.

"Dada, da, baba," Sampson demands when I look down at him, and I bend to pick him up and rest him on my hip.

"No bottle, baby. It's dinnertime," Everly tells him, walking to the round kitchen table and pulling out a high chair that's tucked in the corner.

"No, no, no, baba." He pats my cheek, and his bottom lip starts to wobble.

"Oh, you're good." Everly scoops him out of my arms, then meets my gaze. "And you're a total sucker."

"I didn't do anything."

"You would have. It was written all over your face." She sets him in his seat and buckles him in, then kisses his cheek. "You love peas and pasta." She grabs the plate and dumps some of his food in front of him. He eyes it for a moment, then sweeps his hand across the top of his tray and shoves a handful of food into his mouth. "See? It's yummy."

"Yumm." He rocks back and forth, then holds out a handful of food toward me.

"No thanks, big guy. That's all you." I laugh, then look down at Everly when I feel her gaze on me. When our eyes lock, I'm not sure what the look she's giving me means, and before I can ask her, my cell rings, cutting into the moment. When she turns to take a seat across from Sampson, I pull out my phone and slide my finger across the screen when I see my mom's calling.

"Hey," I answer when I put my phone to my ear.

"Your sister just called to let me know that Everly and Sampson are coming to dinner. Do you know if Sammy is allergic to anything?"

"I'm not sure Everly is coming to dinner, and it's Sampson, not Sammy, Mom," I say, and Everly's head spins around, her wide eyes locking on mine.

"Well, can you call her and ask? I would, but I don't have her cell number, which is ridiculous, since I should have it, and she should have mine."

"Mom wants to know if you're coming to dinner and, if you are, if Sampson is allergic to anything," I say, and both she and Mom gasp at the same time.

"You're with her right now?" Mom asks, sounding a mixture of surprised and happy.

"Yeah," I state simply, watching Everly closely, trying to read what's going on in her head right now.

"Umm . . ." She clears her throat after I raise one brow. "Sam isn't allergic to anything that I know of, and dinner sounds good, if you're sure we won't be imposing."

"Of course she won't be imposing," Mom practically shouts in my ear as Everly holds my gaze captive. "Tell her that and that she's welcome anytime."

"You can tell her tomorrow, Mom. Love you. I'll talk to you later."

"But wait, I—" she sputters as I pull the phone from my ear and hang up the call.

"My mom's excited about dinner."

"Me too." She bites her bottom lip, then asks, "Are you sure it's okay I come?"

"I already told you it was, babe," I assure her, and she nods once, then turns back to Sampson to help him finish eating. When he's done, she makes him a bottle, then unhooks him from his chair. "I'm going to take him up to give him a bath and get him to sleep," she says as he rests his head against her chest. "I shouldn't be long, if you just want to hang down here and watch TV or something."

"I'm good with that," I say, then go to the living room while she heads upstairs. With a little time on my hands, I send out a few texts, then figure I should check the email, but when I open it up, I find everything up to date. I will never admit it to Tanner or Mav, but hiring Everly to work in the office was the smartest thing they ever did. Not only is she great at her job, but she's also brought a lot of great ideas.

"What's that smile for?" Everly asks, coming into the living room, and I set my phone aside to watch her walk toward me, now dressed in a pair of leggings and an oversize long-sleeved T-shirt.

"Nothing." I glance at the baby monitor in her hand. "Is he sleeping?"

"Yes." She laughs. "He started falling asleep the minute I got him in the bath, so I just got him out and dressed, fed him half his bottle, and then laid him down."

"He had a busy day."

"He had a great day." She takes a seat next to me on the couch and smiles. "He's obsessed with you."

"The feeling is mutual. He's a cute kid."

"He's the best," she agrees, then pushes up off the couch when the doorbell rings.

"I got the door," I tell her, figuring it's the pizza, and she nods.

"Do you want a beer or something?"

"I'm good with a beer if you got one." I see her head into the kitchen, and I walk to the front door. After giving the kid who dropped off our food a tip, I take it back to the kitchen and notice her with her cell phone in her hand and a frown on her face as she looks at the screen. "Everything okay?"

"Oh, yeah." She drops the phone facedown on the counter and turns to look at me. "I don't know about you, but I'm starving." Not wanting to call her out for lying, nor piss her off, I set the bags on the table. "Do you feel like watching a movie while we eat?" She moves around the kitchen, avoiding my gaze. "My parents have about every subscription service there is, so I'm sure we can find something to watch."

"That sounds good to me," I tell her, and she nods before handing me a plate and getting one for herself.

After we each have our food, we settle in the living room and end up watching some documentary about a guy who swims in the ocean with an octopus. We continue watching it even after we're finished eating, then move on to a movie about the history of one of the islands off the coast of Florida. She must find it boring or be exhausted, because halfway through the show, she passes out against my side, and instead of waking her up, I wrap my arm around her and settle in.

Blinking my eyes open, it takes a second to remember where I am and another moment to realize the sound that woke me is blaring through the room and coming from the television. It's one of the tests that TV stations send out in the middle of the night. Rubbing my hand down my face, I start to sit up so I can search for the remote but stop when Everly grumbles something, wraps her arms around my waist, and burrows against my chest, her weight feeling like it belongs against me. Just when the emergency test ends, her body against mine grows stiff, letting me know she's awake, and a moment later, she jerks back, making me grunt when her hand collides with my abs, and she pushes away.

"I'm so sorry." She shoves her hair out of her face as she blinks at me. "I can't believe I fell asleep."

"I did too," I tell her, actually surprised; normally there's so much on my mind it takes me hours to drift off.

She looks around the room, seeming a bit dazed. "What time is it?" She gets up off the couch and flips off the TV before turning on one of the lamps.

Glancing into the kitchen, I see the time on the microwave. "Just after one." I get up and pick up the blanket that fell off her at some point, then toss it onto the back of the sofa.

"Sam is going to be up soon." Her eyes come to me, and she tucks some hair behind her ear. "He normally wakes up around two, wanting a bottle before going back to sleep." Her eyes bounce off me as they travel around the room once more. "It's late. Are you going to be okay to drive home?"

"Don't worry about me," I tell her, and she licks her lips, seeming at a loss for what to say or do as I walk into the kitchen to grab my keys off the table.

"You can stay." I turn to face her, and even in the dim light, I notice her cheeks are darker than they were. "I can make up the couch for you, if you want."

"I need to get home. Tutu has been there all day on her own. I'm sure she's wondering where I am."

"You left her all day?" Her eyes are wide, and I smile.

"She has access to the dog door, food, and water, and my neighbors' kid comes to hang with her when I'm out," I assure her, and she visibly relaxes as I walk down the hall toward the front door with her at my side. "Tomorrow, I'll pick you and Sam up, and we'll head to my parents' together." I don't bother making it sound like a suggestion. If she has an out, I know she'll take it, and if I'm going to get her to open up to me, I need to use every opportunity I have available.

"Oh, okay. Sure." She wraps her arms around her middle as I open the door.

"I'll be here at five." I turn to face her, and her eyes drop to my mouth for the briefest of moments.

"See you then," she says quietly, and unable to help myself, I reach out and touch her cheek with the tips of my fingers, then turn and leave.

When I get out to my truck, I find her watching me from the doorway, and even with the space between us, I can see she's at war with herself. One thing I'm learning quickly is that she might be attracted to me, she might like me, and she might even like spending time with me, but it's not going to be easy to get over the wall she's built up to protect herself. The thing she doesn't know is that, in the military, I made a career out of analyzing each obstacle placed between me and whatever it was I wanted, and I was the best at finding a way to reach it in the shortest amount of time.

Chapter 9

EVERLY

With Sampson sitting on the fancy protective cushion that I placed over the shopping cart seat, I walk down the baby aisle at the grocery store, trying to focus on the task at hand. It's something I'm finding more and more difficult to do every time my phone beeps, signaling a new message. Between last night and this morning, Lex has sent me a multitude of texts, each one more hurtful than the previous, and now I'm struggling to figure out if I should even reply.

If he were even a little bit involved in Sam's life, I might feel more inclined to explain to him what happened when we met his mom yesterday, but as things stand, I don't think it would change anything. Time and again, he's made it clear he does not want to be a father, so him telling me that his mother wants him to get a DNA test really does nothing but piss me off. First, because he should know I never, ever would have cheated on him, and second, because the point is moot. Even if Sam weren't his—which he 100 percent is—would it matter? He's never acted like he's his father, never shown any interest in him or his well-being, and he has made it clear he does not want to be involved in any way.

The only reason I'm second-guessing how I should reply is because of my own ego. The fact that he would text things like Do I need to ask you for a DNA test? or My mom said she thinks the guy you brought to meet her and my dad for lunch is Sampson's real dad makes me feel like I need to defend myself. It doesn't matter what he or his mom thinks, does, or says, and they only have power over me if I give it to them. I just need to talk myself out of defending my own virtue.

With a sigh, I stop in front of the diapers, then scan the selection for the brand and size I need while trying to calculate in my head if they're cheaper here or at the store down the street.

"Everly?" I hear my name and look down the aisle, then smile when I see Margret carrying Taylor on her hip, with a very handsome guy pushing a cart right behind her. "I thought that was you." She comes over to give me a one-armed hug, then looks at Sampson. "Hey, buddy, are you having a good day?"

"Nona, baba, dada," he rattles off, making us both laugh.

"I hear you, kid. I feel the same," she tells him as I peek around to Taylor, who's avoiding any kind of attention.

"Hey, pretty girl."

"Hi," she says quietly before she burrows into her mom.

"She just woke up when we got to the store," Margret explains, then motions to the guy a step away. "Everly, I don't know if you've met Mason or not."

"I haven't." I lift my hand and wave at him. "It's nice to meet you."

"You too." He jerks up his chin, then takes Taylor when she reaches out for him to hold her.

"What are you guys up to today?" I ask, looking among the three of them.

"Just doing some shopping, then cleaning and laundry before the week is up and I have to do it all over again."

"Same." I smile, and she smiles back.

"You're coming to Mom and Dad's for dinner, right?"

"Yeah, Blake is picking Sam and me up at five," I tell her, and her eyes start to twinkle, which puts me on edge. I haven't figured out if she either really likes the idea of her brother and me together or if she really likes giving him a hard time.

"Awesome, did you guys have a good day yesterday?" she asks, and I'm not sure how to respond to that question. We did have a great day, or at least I did. I just don't know how he felt, because he's not the easiest guy in the world to read.

"I think so."

"Cool," she says; then her eyes go over my shoulder and narrow. When I turn, I see a very good-looking man with dark hair and timeless features with a gorgeous redheaded woman. The two of them have stopped at the end of the aisle, looking like they've seen a ghost.

"Margret?" Mason rumbles, reaching for her arm, but she shakes him off and storms past me.

"I cannot believe you," she hisses, approaching the couple, and the woman backs behind the man while he holds up his hands.

"Margret, this is not the time or place to cause a scene," the guy with dark hair says as Margret stomps toward him.

"You are a liar." She shoves her finger in his face. "I cannot believe you."

"Calm down," he orders, and even with Margret's back to me, I can tell by the sudden stiffness in her shoulders that she doesn't like him telling her to calm down. Then again, what woman likes it when a man says that?

"Do not tell me to calm down." She tosses her hands in the air, then points at the woman, who's attempting to blend in with the baby formula. "Let me guess—you just so happened to run into him here."

"Umm." She looks around like she's confused, and I hear Mason sigh. Then his hand lands on my shoulder, and I turn to face him and notice that Taylor looks upset.

"Daddy," she says, and for a moment, I think she's talking to Mason, but then I realize she's looking at the man Margret is arguing with.

"Everly." Mason pulls my attention back to him and holds out some cash in my direction. "Will you take Taylor to the café at the front of the store to get something to eat?"

"Daddy," Taylor repeats, sounding upset, and my eyes ping between her and the man at the end of the aisle, who's obviously her father and Margret's ex.

"It's okay, pumpkin," the man says to Taylor, and Margret's hands ball into fists while the redheaded woman seems to pale.

"It's okay, honey." Margret spins on her heel and walks back to us, then takes Taylor from Mason.

"Daddy." She reaches for her father, and Margret looks like she wants to cry or physically hurt someone.

"Hey, pumpkin." He walks over, giving Mason a weary look before he takes Taylor from her mom. "Are you having a good day with Mommy?" he asks, and she says something I can't really make out, because it's a mixture of baby talk and words that are almost whispered.

"She had been looking forward to spending the day with you today," Margret tells him softly while touching Taylor's hair.

"Sorry, pumpkin. Something came up." He kisses the top of Taylor's head. I chew on my bottom lip, feeling awkward and angry on Margret and Taylor's behalf, because my guess is what "came up" is the redhead, who took off when he came over to comfort his daughter. One good thing Lex did was make it clear he had no desire to be a dad. Yes, I had hoped and convinced myself that he would change, but I was not surprised when he didn't.

Watching this situation, I'm happy Sam won't have to go through this kind of disappointment. Not to say that one day he's not going to have some hard questions for me to answer about his father, but I hope it's at a time when he can really understand the full scope of the situation.

"We need to go," Margret says, and I can't tell if her ex looks relieved or disappointed when she takes Taylor from him.

"Sure." He steps back and tucks his hands into the front pockets of his jeans. "I'll call you and let you know when I can pick her up this week."

"Whatever," she mutters under her breath before looking at me. "I'll see you tonight, Everly."

"Yeah." I clear my throat. "I'll see you tonight." With a jerk of her chin, she takes off with Taylor in her arms, and Mason walks next to her with his arm around her waist, pushing the shopping cart with one hand.

"Sorry about that," her ex says to me as they disappear around the corner, and I frown at him. "She gets a little crazy sometimes."

"Does she?" I ask sarcastically, but he must not catch it, because he runs his fingers through his hair and smiles what I'm sure is his most charming smile.

"Yeah."

"Well, maybe she wouldn't act 'crazy'"—I make air quotes—"if you didn't make her that way." I hold up my hand when it looks like he's going to speak. "What I saw just a second ago is a mom who wants the father of her child to spend time with his daughter and is confused why he doesn't want the same thing." I grab hold of my cart, then toss my hair over my shoulder. "Good day to you, sir." I storm off, then press my lips together, thinking that I really need to stop reading so many historical romances.

~

With Sam napping and laundry going, I step out onto my parents' back porch with the baby monitor. I set it on the small side table next to the couch and take a seat, wishing it wasn't too early to drink, because I could totally do with a shot of tequila right about now. After having the day to think things over, I decided that I should call Lex and clear the air rather than text so there's no confusion. After dialing his number, I put the phone on speaker and listen to it ring, hoping secretly that he doesn't answer, and I can say I tried.

"Everly." He picks up, sounding like he's out of breath.

"Hey." I stand up and walk to the edge of the porch that overlooks my parents' small overgrown back yard.

"Did you get my messages?" he asks, and I roll my eyes skyward.

"I did, which is why I needed some time to think about how I would respond."

"How you would respond?" He sounds confused.

"About you asking if you need to get a DNA test," I remind him, and I hear him moving around. "I needed to think about how to respond to that kind of question, since you know I never cheated on you, and you also know I never pressured you into being a father."

"You had a baby, Everly. What more pressure did I need?" he asks, and a spark of anger starts in my lower belly.

"I did have a baby, Lex, a baby you have not had one thing to do with."

"I told you I didn't want to be a father."

"I know, which is why I haven't asked you to step up to the plate to be there, neither emotionally nor financially."

"My mom is convinced that the guy you brought with you to meet her is his real father," he says, and I want to tell him exactly what I think of his mother, but I know nothing I say would be very nice, so I swallow the urge down. I do not want to argue with him. I don't even want to talk to him, but I know I need to get this done with.

"I didn't know Blake until I moved home and got a job. He's my boss," I tell him. "When you and I were together, I was always with you, so you should know there was never a time for me to step out on you."

"You worked and I worked, so we were not always together, and we used condoms, so I still don't know how you got pregnant to begin with."

"I'm pretty sure it says right on the box that condoms are only ninety-nine percent effective, so it's my guess that we were one of the lucky one percent of people they failed for," I tell him, then shake my head. "Anyway, what does it matter? You don't want to be a father, and I'm okay with that. As far as I'm concerned, we don't ever have to speak again."

"If he's mine, my mom wants to know him," he says, and that anger in the pit of my stomach turns from a small flame to an inferno, because once more, he's not saying he wants to be involved; he just wants his mother to have the option.

"He is biologically yours, Lex. With that said, I do not want your mother around my son after the way she acted."

"She's just trying to protect me," he grumbles, and my nostrils flare. I swear if he were in front of me, I might be tempted to wrap my hands around his neck.

"And I'm protecting my child, who cannot protect himself, and I do not want your mother in his life." I let out a breath and count backward from ten to hopefully get my temper under control.

"So I'm going to have to get a DNA test?" he asks, and I see red.

"Yes, you are going to have to pay to get a DNA test; then you are going to have to serve me with papers, ordering me to take my son to get one; then, once the results come back and they prove you are the father, you are going to have to take me to court and force me to let your mom see my child. And in the meantime, I'm going to take you to court for child support, including back child support, since you have not given me one cent for Sam since the day he was born. So I figure you're going to be a year behind by the time this is all settled, so you might want to start saving now."

"Jesus, Everly, what the fuck?"

"Do not *what the fuck* me, Lex. This isn't my idea. This is yours. I'm not the one asking you to be involved in Sam's life. You are not even the one who wants to be involved in Sam's life. You are asking me to allow your mother to be a part of my child's life after I prove what we both already know, and had she not acted the way she did when we met her, I would have been all about him getting to know his grandparents. Now, not so much, so if you want to force me to have Sam take a test or to get to know your mom, I want you to know you are going to have a fight on your hands. I'm giving you fair warning and just letting you know that you need to be ready to go to battle with me."

I wait, breathing heavily, for him to say something, anything, and when he doesn't, I tap the screen to make sure the call is still connected. It is, which means he's at a loss for words, probably not realizing what kind of repercussions him doing this might have.

"If that's all, I need to get off the phone. I have things I need to get done."

"Yeah" is all he says, and when he doesn't say more after a moment, I hang up. I probably could have been a little nicer, but the truth is, I'm done being nice. There is only one person in this entire fucked-up situation who could get hurt, and that's Sam, and he cannot defend himself, so it's my job to do that until he's able to—and even then, long after that.

After a few deep breaths, I grab the baby monitor and head inside to finish cleaning up the house and doing laundry, while trying to figure out what I'm going to tell my parents tonight when they get home. Neither of them knew I was meeting with Lex's parents, something I didn't tell them about, because if I did, they would have delayed their trip to see my brother, and I know they were looking forward to seeing him and his family.

Part of me still doesn't want to bring it up to them, but honestly, I'm worried that Lex is going to force my hand, and I'll be left with no other choice but to depend on my parents to help me once again. I just really hope it doesn't come to that.

Once my list of things to get done is complete, I wake up Sam and give him a snack, then take him upstairs with me so I can get us both ready to go to Blake's parents' house. Needing to keep Sam occupied and mostly contained, I place him in his bouncer and move it next to the bathroom door so I can keep an eye on him while I do my makeup and hair.

I used to think when he was a tiny baby how awesome it would be when he was able to move around, but now I realize I took that time for granted. Getting him to stay still or in one place nowadays is almost impossible, which makes it a production whenever I need to do a normal task like get ready for work or to go out.

As I finish up my makeup, the anxiousness I was feeling most of the day is replaced with giddiness, and try as I might, I can't help but be excited to spend time with Blake. After I'm ready, I put on a black tank and a pair of black leggings, then grab a long cream sweater that goes almost to my knees, the color the same as the wedge booties I plan on wearing tonight. Once I'm dressed, I go back through the bathroom and into his room to get his outfit from his closet—a buffalo plaid button-down shirt and jeans that my mom bought for him from one of the shops in town.

With how wiggly he is, it takes me more than a few minutes to get him dressed, and I swear I need a shower when I'm finished. Once I've finally wrestled him into his clothes, I scoop him up and take him downstairs, where I place him in front of the TV so I can get his bag packed.

Just when I've got his bottle made and some snacks shoved into one of the side pockets in case he doesn't want anything Janet makes, the doorbell rings. Butterflies erupt in my stomach, letting me know the crush I know I should not have on him is still very much alive.

"Sam, Blake is here," I tell my boy, and he turns to look at me and smiles, then gets up off the ground and starts to waddle toward me. I scoop him up and take him with me to the door, and as soon as I open it, he reaches for Blake, gurgling something I can't make out.

"I missed you, too, big guy." Blake kisses his cheek while stepping into the house, and I try to talk my heart out of melting, but it's no use.

I can tell myself all day long that I'm not interested in him as anything more than a friend, but the truth is, I do like him. I like how he treats my son. I like the way he looks at me, and I like how I feel when I'm around him. Is he the most happy-go-lucky guy I've ever met? No. But maybe that is not as important as I've always thought it was. Maybe it's more important to be solid, stable, and dependable, not the life of the party and the charming guy who always wants to have a good time.

"You look beautiful."

His comment takes a moment to register, but when it does, those butterflies fly faster and heat spreads up my neck to my cheeks and down to the bottom of my stomach.

"Thank you." Our eyes lock, and a different kind of feeling spreads through me. "I . . ." I clear my throat when I realize how husky my voice sounds. "I just need to grab his bag; then we can go."

"No rush. I came a few minutes early so I could help you get him ready if you needed it."

"Oh," I say quietly, once again caught off guard by his thoughtfulness. "He's ready, but I do need to get his car seat set up in your truck if you're driving."

"I bought a car seat today. It's all hooked up," he tells me, and I blink. "I figured that between him and Taylor, it would be good if I got one for my truck."

"Right," I agree, totally taken aback for the third time since he's been here. "Then I guess we can leave." I grab Sam's bag, and he gets close, sliding the bag off my shoulder.

"Are you okay?" he asks me softly, and when our gazes meet, I have the sudden urge to hug him and tell him everything. Each time I've been in his arms, I've felt safe, something I haven't felt in a while—not with everything happening. I just don't know if I should place him in a situation where I'm not only depending on him to sign my paychecks but also to comfort me when I need it.

"Great," I tell him, and he eyes me doubtfully. "It's just been a weird day." I wave off his concern.

"Weird how?" he asks, and I shrug. "I ran into your sister and a friend of hers at the store, then watched her have it out with her ex. Then, when I—"

"Margret had it out with Taylor's dad at the store?"

"No . . . I mean, kind of. It wasn't a *fight* fight. I just don't think she expected to see him there, so when she did, she got upset."

"Sundays are his day to spend with Taylor," he tells me—something I already kind of figured out. "He must have canceled, which he does, and normally it's to spend time with other women, which makes it worse."

"He was there with a redhead," I tell him, and his eyes narrow. "Or I think they were there together. She didn't hang around very long."

"There is only one redhead I know, and that's Margret's friend Beth, so I hope it wasn't her."

"I don't know," I tell him, even though I'm pretty sure from the way Margret reacted to seeing them together it was her friend—or probably now her ex-friend.

"I'll ask her about it at dinner." He turns for the door, and my eyes widen.

Reaching out quickly, I latch onto his T-shirt and shake my head when he looks at me over his shoulder. "You can't do that."

"Pardon?" His brows dart together.

"You can't tell her that I told you about what happened."

"Why not?"

"She might not want you to know, for one, and for two, she will know I told you."

"She won't care that you told me." He frowns, and I roll my eyes.

"You can't be serious." I shake my head at him. "She will care if she didn't plan on telling you about it."

"She won't." He sighs, reaching around and grabbing my hand before pulling me with him down the front hall to the entryway.

"Does she tell you everything?" I ask, stopping to lock the door when we get outside, and when he doesn't respond, I answer for him. "I have an older brother, and I don't tell him everything, so I'm going to go with no, she doesn't tell you everything either."

"We're close."

"I don't doubt that, but you keep things from her, so you shouldn't be surprised if she keeps things from you," I tell him, and he lets out a long sigh and takes my hand once more. When we get to the truck, he opens my door, ordering me to get in before he puts Sam in the seat in the back, a seat that's nicer than even the one I own.

"Are you nervous about dinner?" He turns to look at me after he's got his seat belt on, and I shrug.

"Not really. Should I be?"

"No, you know my sister and my mom, and my dad's cool, so you'll love him. I'm not sure if my grandmother or one of my childhood friends, Mason, will be there tonight, but if they are, you'll like them too."

"I met Mason today at the store. He was with Margret," I tell him as he pulls out into the road, and he glances my way, looking unhappy.

"He was with Margret?"

"Why are you asking that question like I should say no?" I turn around to check on Sam and give him the duck toy that's hooked on the outside of his bag. "Please tell me that you're not still telling your friends they can't like your sister."

"I never said that," he says defensively.

I don't even try to hide my smile. "Right."

"I haven't."

"Okay, so what would you do if one of your friends started dating Margret?" I ask, honestly curious, because Margret is young, pretty, and sweet. And from what I could see today, Mason is protective of her and is around Taylor enough that she took comfort in his presence during a difficult situation between her parents. I mean, I don't know what is going on between them, but I could definitely see them together.

"Not going to happen." He waves the question off, and I laugh. "You think that's funny?"

"No, I just think you don't have as much control as you think you do. And anyways, if one of your friends and your sister got together and made each other happy, you should be happy for them," I tell him, and he doesn't say anything more about it.

Actually, he's surprisingly quiet as we drive out of town and up the side of the mountain, where the houses are spread farther apart. He turns down a paved driveway with forest on both sides and a beautiful log home at the end of it. Having met his mom, I should've been able to picture the house she would own, because it looks as warm and inviting as she is in person. The lights inside the house are glowing, making the windows golden, and planters of flowers leading up the large front porch are overflowing with color. As he parks, the front door opens and his mom steps outside, followed by a man who's just as tall and attractive as Blake.

Without waiting for him, I open my door and get out, then open the back door of the truck and get in to retrieve Sam from his seat. When I have him in my arms, I turn to get out but stop when I find Blake standing just inside the open door.

"You're right," he tells me quietly, taking Sam when he reaches for him. "Margret deserves to be happy, even if that's with one of my friends."

I want to tell him how proud of him I am, because I know how big him admitting that is, but I don't. Instead, I take his hand and let him help me down out of his truck.

"Oh my goodness, aren't you just the cutest?" Janet gushes over Sampson, and he starts to babble and laugh as she leans up to kiss Blake's cheek; then her eyes come to me. "Hi, sweetheart." She looks over her shoulder at her husband. "Dave, honey, this is Everly. Everly, this is my Dave," she tells me, and my nose starts to sting.

Okay, maybe me being here isn't such a good idea, because hearing her call her husband *my Dave* is almost too much to take when I know the secret he's forcing his son to keep.

Blake's hand lands warm against my lower back, then slides to curve around my hip like he knows I might lose it.

"It's nice to meet you," I tell Dave, and his eyes drop to his son's hand before meeting mine and warming.

"Nice to meet you, too, Everly. I've heard a lot about you."

"Oh no." I make a face, and he laughs.

"All good things, I promise," he says as Sam lunges for him, and he takes him easily.

"That's good."

"I'd say so." He then turns back to the house and looks down at Sam. "Do you like trains? Taylor is already inside playing with the train I set up," he says, and Sam babbles what sounds like the word *train* and kicks his tiny feet in excitement.

"I hope you're hungry." Janet links her arm with mine, and as Blake's hand drops away, I instantly miss his touch. "I might have gone a little overboard with dinner tonight."

"When don't you go overboard?" Blake asks, and she looks around me just so she can glare at him. "Never mind."

"I thought so," she mutters, and I laugh as we head into the house, which is just as warm and welcoming as the outside. Art and photos of friends and family line the walls, and rugs cover the wood floor all the way down the hall. When we enter the main room, with the kitchen on one side and the living room on the other, I find Dave has already settled Sam on the floor with Taylor. They're between the couch and fireplace in the middle of a large oval train track that has a LEGO train going around it, pulling cars with different animals behind it.

"Hey, Everly." Margret gets off the couch to greet me with a hug, then whispers against my ear, "I'm sorry about today."

"It's okay." I hug her tighter. "Are you okay?"

"Absolutely," she whispers, then lets me go and plasters a smile on her face. "How are you and the grump doing?"

"We're friends, so we're good," I tell her; then we both look at Sam when he starts shouting "Da, da, da, da." Of course Blake takes that as his cue, and the minute he picks him up, Sam rests his tiny head against Blake's shoulder, and Dave smiles at his son.

"Friends," Margret repeats as we both watch her brother hold Sam. "Keep telling yourself that, girl." Since I have no comeback, I go into the kitchen and ask if Janet needs help, and when she says no, I go hang in the living room with Dave, who is soft spoken, witty, and undeniably charming.

As the evening carries on, I realize that Blake is the man he is because of his family, and being around them, I understand him a little more than I did before. I also see he is the kind of guy who wants everyone around him to be happy, even if that happiness comes at his own expense.

Chapter 10

EVERLY

Holding my breath, I wait for my mom to respond to what I've just told her about Lex, his mom, and everything that happened while she and Dad were gone.

"I cannot believe you didn't call me," my mom whispers, and I chew my bottom lip. "You should have told me that you had plans to meet with Lex's mom and dad, and you really should have told me what happened after you met with them."

Hating the disappointment I hear in her voice, I avoid eye contact and focus on getting Sampson to eat his breakfast. "I didn't want you and Dad to cancel your plans. I knew you two had been looking forward to going to see Jayson, Meg, and the kids. I didn't want you to cancel that because of me."

"You could have postponed meeting them, Everly."

"I wanted to get it over with." I meet her gaze. "I just wanted it done, and to be honest, I forgot you and Dad were going away, so I didn't want to ask them for a rain check, and I didn't want to tell you about the plans I made."

"I guess." She tucks her feet up under her on the chair she's sitting on, then picks up her coffee. "I just hate that you went through that after everything you've already gone through."

"I hate it, too, but it's done. Now I have to wait and see what Lex is going to do. He hasn't changed his mind about being a part of Sam's life, so if he does serve me with papers to have Sam tested, I know it's got nothing to do with him and everything to do with his mom."

"I didn't think they were close."

"I didn't think so, either, but when it comes to Lex, I'm learning I have no idea who he really is."

"Yeah." She eyes Sam thoughtfully. "I'm not making excuses for Lex's mom, and I know Sam is not Blake's, but they do look a lot alike," she says. Sam, hearing Blake's name, starts to repeat "Da, da, da" over and over again, and Mom gives me a look.

"He doesn't know what he's saying," I remind her. "And I could walk down the street and find ten guys who look like they could be Sam's dad."

"You're right, I suppose." She puts her feet on the floor and gets up. "I'm glad Blake was there for you."

"Yeah, me too," I agree quietly, and she leans over to kiss the top of my head and then tucks a strand of hair behind my ear when she leans back, meeting my gaze.

"Whatever happens, your dad and I will support you."

"Thanks, Mom," I say quietly, and she nods.

"I'm going to get dressed so you can take off."

"Cool." I let out a deep breath, and she nods once before disappearing around the corner, out of the kitchen.

"Mama." Sam pats my arm, and I focus on him. "Da, da, da." He looks around, and I laugh.

"Blake is at his house, baby."

"No." He pouts, and I grab my phone and snap a picture of him, then text it to Blake, telling him that Sam is pouting because he's not around, figuring he will think it's cute. Just when I start to put my cell down, it rings with Blake's name, saying he's video calling. My chest warms as I slide my finger across the screen.

"Hey." I smile when his handsome, sweaty face appears a moment later. "I'm guessing you're calling to talk to this guy." I flip the phone around to Sam, and he takes the phone from me, putting his mouth against the screen as he babbles, and I listen to Blake laugh.

A couple of minutes later, when Blake asks if he can talk to Mommy, I wrestle my cell away from Sam, then wipe off the front, which is now covered with slobber and baby cereal. "Sorry about that," I tell him when I hold the phone up to my face.

"Don't apologize." He drops the phone to a surface so that I'm looking at the ceiling; then I hear the whoosh of fabric and the sound of water turning on. When he picks the phone back up, I can see he's now shirtless, and my stomach dips. "Sucks I won't be able to spend much time with you two this week, with the clients coming in today," he tells me, looking like he really does think it sucks, and that warmth in my chest spreads through me. "We'll make plans for the weekend. Maybe we can go back to Kirk's farm and then have dinner at my place."

"I like that idea," I say, and his expression softens. Damn, but I really do like this guy.

"All right, babe, I'm gonna get in the shower, then head to work. I'll see you there."

"See you there," I agree.

He hangs up after a quick "Later," and I set my phone on the table, then feed Sam the rest of his cereal and clean him up before passing him off to my mom.

I run upstairs and get dressed, since I already did my hair and makeup before Sam woke up; then I run back downstairs and kiss both my mom and boy goodbye. On the drive to the lodge, I wonder if I shouldn't tread more carefully in this situation with Blake. He already has a lot on his plate, with his dad and his business. Then you add in Sampson and me, and I wonder if it's all too much for him. And even though I wish I wouldn't just be disappointed or seriously hurt if things were to go sour between us, I know I would be. I just hope that I'm not wrong about him.

~

As I sit in front of my computer, trying to get everything prepared for the guests who should be here any minute, I feel Maverick staring at me and sigh. "What?"

"Nothing," he mutters, and I take my eyes off the computer to look at him and see a smirk on his face that he's not even attempting to hide.

"Seriously, spit it out or get out of my office. I have stuff to do," I tell him, and he grins a very smug, very amused grin.

"I hope all the time you're spending with Blake doesn't make you as cranky as he is," he says, and heat spreads up my neck to my cheeks. "Margret told me that you two had lunch together Saturday and you went to his parents' for dinner Sunday. Sucks I missed that."

"Well, aren't you just Little Miss *Gossip Girl*?" I snap, and he chuckles.

"I'm happy for you both," he says, and I frown at him, then look at the door and watch Blake walk in, carrying two cups of coffee, a smile on his face. Darn, but seeing him, I swear my entire body lights up.

"What's up, man?" he asks Maverick, and the two of them share a chin lift; then he sets one of the mugs on the desk in front of me and meets my gaze. "Mom told me how you take it."

"Thanks." I pick it up and take a sip as he sits in one of the chairs across from me.

"Where's my coffee?" Maverick asks.

"In the kitchen," he tells him.

"Right." Maverick grins, then stands. "I'm gonna grab a cup; then I'll meet you two in the front so we can greet the guests when they arrive."

"The bus will be here in less than ten minutes," I tell him after glancing at the clock on the wall. "The driver called from the hotel and told me that he was going to be on his way about fifteen minutes ago."

"It was smart of you to suggest busing them in, baby," Blake says.

"Yeah, it was, babe," Maverick agrees, and Blake sends him a narrowed-eye look, which I ignore.

"Thanks." I smile at them. Normally, guests don't arrive here by bus or in a group, but because there were so many people coming in for the bachelor/bachelorette party, I suggested we hire transportation to bring them to the lodge from the hotel they were all staying at near the airport. None of the guys seemed to think it was necessary, but they let me do what I thought was best, so I ran with it and am happy to see they think it was a good idea.

"All right, I'm gonna go to the kitchen. I'll meet you both out front," Maverick says. Once he's gone, Blake relaxes back in his chair, and I go back to typing the email I was in the middle of writing. Just as with Maverick, I can feel his eyes on me, but the feeling I get from him watching me is different.

"You're staring at me," I say quietly, glancing at him out of the corner of my eye.

"I like your hair like that," he replies, and I lift my hand automatically to touch the twist I put my hair up into this morning.

"Thanks." I bite my bottom lip.

"Are you ready for today?"

I turn to face him after I send off the email and shrug one shoulder.

"I think so. I mean, I'm not really doing anything but handing out some pamphlets and answering questions. You and Maverick are the ones who are going to have your work cut out for you, judging by the emails I've received over the last couple of weeks." I smile. "One person asked how much it would cost them to have us build a shower at each campsite, and another was seriously disappointed when I told them that we would not be supplying mattresses for guests to sleep on and could not understand why we couldn't just take a U-Haul up the mountain." I shake my head. "I have a feeling that even the ones who think they're ready for the next few days are going to realize they're not."

"You're probably right about that, but then again, the good tends to outweigh the bad after the first night. I mean, yeah, you have to sleep on the ground, but you get to spend the night under the stars, like you've never seen them before. You have to wake up at the crack of dawn; then you get to watch the sunrise. You have to walk for miles; then you get to spend hours in a kayak going down one of the most beautiful rivers in the United States."

"I guess that's one way to look at it," I say, and he smiles a smile that makes my toes curl.

"Have you gone camping before?"

"No, like I told you before, I'm not really an outdoorsy kinda girl."

"We'll have to go at least once this summer," he says, and hope fills my chest, because if he's talking about us spending time together in the future, that might mean that he sees in me what I see in him. "One thing I've learned is no one is ever happy to step outside their comfort zone, but they do tend to really fucking enjoy it after they've stepped over that line." He stands with his coffee before I can respond and asks, "Are you finished in here?"

"Yeah." I glance at the computer and the dozens of emails we got over the weekend. "Or for now I am."

"Then let's go out front and wait for everyone."

I push back my chair, grab the coffee he brought me, and walk out of the office ahead of him. When we get to the main room in the lodge, I see that Janet has been hard at work this morning. Not only is there fresh coffee and tea in large heated metal pots, but there's also an assortment of muffins, danishes, and fresh fruit, along with meats and cheeses, set up on a long table, with plates, cups, silverware, and napkins on the end.

"Your mom needs a raise."

"Believe me, she doesn't," Blake says, and I eye him questioningly. "Maverick, Tanner, and I offered her over four times what she was making at her last job, and she does half the work with little to no stress."

"She's worth it."

"You're right; she is, and if she asked for more, we'd give it to her." He places his hand against my lower back and urges me down the hall toward the front door. When we step outside onto the porch, I spot Maverick at the back of his Jeep, pulling out a backpack that looks to be about as big as I am. Then I turn when I hear people shouting.

"Oh my goodness," I whisper, hearing Blake curse behind me as the bus drives into the lot with all the windows down and people hanging out, with white streamers and Silly String shooting out like confetti and covering the ground. "Are they drunk?"

"I fucking hope not," Maverick grumbles, coming up the steps to where we're standing.

"If they are, we are not taking them out today," Blake says, and I nod my agreement. I don't even want to imagine the kind of disaster that would ensue from taking a whole group of drunk people on a hike up a mountain on a hot day like today.

When the door to the bus opens, I blink as a blonde in a white tank proclaiming she's the *Bride to Be*, a pair of white leggings, a white fluffy tulle skirt, and sneakers gets off the bus. She's followed by a much older gentleman wearing a T-shirt that looks like a tux, and the rest of their group emerges after them. All the men and women are dressed much the same as the leading couple. When the doors start to close, a girl younger than everyone else, dressed in black with dark hair, fights them open, then stumbles off the bottom step, the weight of her backpack almost toppling her over.

"What the fuck." Maverick starts to step forward but seems to stop himself when she turns to say something to the driver, who's still on the bus. She then walks off to stand alone away from everyone, looking like she would rather be anywhere else.

"Hi." The blonde wearing the *Bride* tank top approaches us while waving, the man at her side looking happy but nowhere near as thrilled as she does. Having chatted with them over email and on the phone a few times, I know the older gentleman must be Oliver, and his fiancée is Lauren.

"Please tell me that we charged them double for this," Maverick says under his breath, and I can't help but smile.

"We're so happy to be back here," Lauren says as she heads right for Maverick, wrapping her arms around him in a hug that obviously makes him uncomfortable. When she does the same with Blake, I almost want to laugh at the look on his face. "We saw that Cybil and Tanner had their baby. You can't imagine how happy we are for both of them," she says when she lets Blake go; then she looks at me. "She and I follow each other on social media."

"Awesome." I smile, and she leans into me.

"Just imagine—she and I both got our happily ever afters, after a couples retreat right here." She points at the ground.

"Imagine that," I agree, and she holds her hand out toward me, the huge rock on her finger glittering in the early-morning sun.

"Sorry, my manners are failing me this morning. I'm Lauren, and this handsome guy here is my soon-to-be husband, Oliver."

"It's nice to meet you both in person. I'm Everly; we've been in touch a few times over email and on the phone." I let go of her hand and take Oliver's when he holds it out.

"Everly, I don't know why I thought you'd be much older," Lauren says; then she looks around, and a second later, her eyes land on the girl standing a few feet away from everyone. "Ozzie, come here!" she shouts, and Maverick tenses next to me.

Ozzie looks less than happy about being summoned, and as she gets closer, I realize that she's not a girl but a woman my age or just a couple of years younger.

"Yes?" Ozzie raises a brow, and Lauren's smile slips ever so slightly.

"I just wanted you to tell them about the sleeping situation," she says, and Ozzie lets out a long breath.

"Lauren, I already told you it's fine. I'll stay with Jake; it's not a big deal."

"Please stop calling me Lauren; I'm your mom, and you said he makes you uncomfortable," she reminds her quietly, and Oliver frowns.

"This whole thing makes me uncomfortable." She looks around. "But who knows? Maybe Jake won't even show up."

"Of course he'll show up." Oliver sighs.

"He didn't make it on the bus this morning."

"He was up late, working."

"I'm sure," she mumbles, rolling her eyes at Oliver, and he looks like he's going to say something, but before he can open his mouth, I cut in.

"I'm sure we can work something out." I glance between Blake and Maverick quickly, hoping I'm not overstepping but also not caring if I am. No way would I want to share a tent with a man who made me uncomfortable. "If you're not comfortable sharing a tent, we will give you your own."

"Babe." Blake rests his hand against my lower back, and I turn to him. "We don't have enough tents for that."

"We don't?" I frown at him, and his eyes drop to my mouth, making my pulse race.

"I'll bunk with Jake," Maverick says, and Ozzie looks up at him, and when her eyes widen, I can only guess that she didn't notice him before. Maybe she didn't; Maverick tends to blend in with the background when he doesn't want to be seen.

"Oh my." She shakes her head while her cheeks turn a pretty shade of pink. "T . . . that's not necessary. It's really not a big deal."

"Then it won't be a big deal that you take my tent," he says; then he looks at the other couples gathered around. "Let's all head inside. We have breakfast set up, and while you eat, we can go over the schedule for the next few days." Then, seeming a lot like Blake, he turns without another word and heads up the steps. I watch him go inside and then look at Ozzie, who's wearing a look of confusion and embarrassment.

"Come on, honey." Lauren takes her arm and leads her inside, with Oliver and the rest of the group following suit.

"Was that weird?" I turn to ask Blake, and he pulls his gaze off the door and drops his eyes to me.

"Yeah."

"I thought so," I mumble. "How do we not have enough tents?"

"This is the largest group we've had at one time. We figured that the five we have on hand would be more than enough. I hadn't thought about ordering more."

"Right. I'll put in an order tomorrow. We should have at least a couple extra in case one of them breaks or something," I say, and he smiles like he thinks I'm being funny. "What?"

"Tents don't normally break, baby."

"Fine—rips or whatever." I roll my eyes at him and head up the steps to the lodge door, ignoring his laughter and just how much I like him calling me *babe* and *baby*.

When we make it to the main room, I see that everyone's started helping themselves to food and drinks, so I go to the television on the wall and grab the remote. Over the last week, whenever I had a minute of free time, I worked on putting together a slide show of pictures that guests have taken while on retreats or guided tours with the guys. I added music, figuring that—if nothing else—it would be good background noise when people were visiting the lodge. When I press play, the first image that comes up is a photo Cybil took, one of the many photos I noticed on the walls of her and Tanner's house. A beautiful view of a valley and waterfall, with the sky above changing from darkness to dusk.

"Did you do this?" Blake asks, coming to stand next to me.

"I did." I tip my head back and smile up at him. "Do you like it?"

"Yeah." His gaze wanders over my face; then his eyes catch on my mouth, and my stomach dips as heat pings between us. I swear I feel him get closer, but the moment is broken when someone shouts.

"You made it!"

We both turn to see who's arrived, and I know immediately that the guy who looks like he just walked out of a college frat house must be Jake. No wonder Ozzie doesn't want to share a tent with him. The arrogant look on his face screams that he's used to getting what he wants, and his pink polo is tucked into his shorts with his collar popped, screaming *pompous jerk*.

"I would have been here earlier, but no one woke me up." He scans the room, and I see him focus on Ozzie, who looks less than happy about his presence. Obviously not feeling the love, he takes his eyes off her and looks around, smiling at the other people in the group, who all smile back. As Oliver joins him and motions for him to go make himself something to eat, I glance to where Maverick is standing. If I hadn't gotten to know him over the last few weeks, I wouldn't notice the tight set of his jaw as he watches Jake.

"While everyone's eating, I'm going to run to the office to grab the stuff I laminated," I tell Blake, hearing him say "Sure" before I quickly make my exit. As I get to my desk, I notice my cell phone is lit up, so I grab it to check and make sure I don't have a missed call from my mom or any messages from her. When I look at the screen, I find a message from a number I don't recognize. I slide my finger across the screen to open it up, and my heart sinks as I read a text from Lex's mother. It informs me that she has spoken with a lawyer, and they will be in contact, since she is going to be filing for grandparents' rights.

It takes me a few minutes to gather my composure, and once I'm sure I won't break down, I collect the box I came to retrieve with all the pamphlets and safety information for the retreat. I'm holding on by a thread as I head back to the main room, and with my head spinning, I hurry down the hall in a rush, really wanting to get back to Blake.

I know now isn't the time to tell him everything that's happened, but being near him seems to always make me feel better, and now more than ever, I could use his strength.

Just before I turn the corner into the main room, the box I'm carrying is shoved into my chest, causing the air to leave my lungs in a rush and me to stumble back a step.

"Darn, I'm so sorry," a man says, taking hold of my arms holding the box, and I blink as I come face-to-face with Jake. "Or maybe I'm not sorry." His eyes roam over me while he grins.

Fighting the curl of my lip, I take a step back from him, and thankfully he lets me go. "It's okay." I step to the left to go around him, and he moves into my path.

"Do you need help?" He reaches for the box, and I shake my head.

"Thanks, I got it." I step to the right, and he follows, blocking my way once more.

"Are you sure?"

"Yes." I plaster a fake smile on my face, because he is a guest, then tip my head to the side. "Can you please move?"

He doesn't move. Instead, he takes a step toward me, making me really understand why Ozzie doesn't want to be around him. "What's your name?"

"No guests are allowed back here," Blake says sharply, and I breathe a sigh of relief when he comes into view, his face a mask of thunder.

"Sorry, man, I was looking for the restroom," Jake tells him, then turns to me and winks. *Barf.* "See you around." He turns and saunters off, and the tension in my shoulders relaxes.

"Are you okay?" Blake comes to stand in front of me, taking the box from my hold, and I nod, then shake my head. "Did he touch you?" The anger in his tone is like a physical thing swirling in the air around us.

"No, he just wouldn't get out of my way," I assure him, knowing right then that even if the answer were yes, I would still say no, because he looks ready to kill someone. And as much as I don't like Jake right now, I really do not like the idea of Blake going to jail for kicking his ass, especially when I don't have enough money to bail him out.

"Okay." His entire being seems to relax. "Are you sure you're okay?"

"I'm sure," I lie, because I might be okay about what just happened, but I'm definitely not all right. The fact that I might be forced to let Lex's mother spend time with my baby is like a knife to my gut.

"All right." He leans into me, and before I know what he's doing, he touches his lips to mine in a soft, closed-mouth kiss that's over before it even begins. "Come on." He transfers the box to carry it under his arm, then takes my hand in his, lacing our fingers together.

Still in a complete daze, I let him lead me to the main room of the lodge. Then, for the next two hours, I try to appear professional as I replay that kiss over and over again in my head. All thoughts of Lex, his mom, and the drama swirling around my life are a distant memory.

Chapter 11

EVERLY

With early-morning light shining through the window and Sampson sitting on my lap, I point at a picture of a black dog and listen to him say the word *dog* in his cute little voice. It comes out more like *bog*.

"Good job, baby." I flip the page to the image of a car. "What's this?"

"Car."

"And this?" I flip to the last page.

"Fuck," he says, referring to the duck, and I laugh as I drop the book to the carpet, then wrap my arms around him and rock him back and forth as I kiss his cheek, making him giggle.

"You're so smart." I fall to my back and lift him up so that he's flying in the air above me, and he smiles, showing off his top two teeth that are now fully through his gums, making him even more adorable. "What do we say we go eat breakfast now?" I ask him, and he rattles off something I'm guessing is his agreement, causing a long string of drool to roll off his bottom lip.

Before it can hit me in the face, I sit up and grab a wipe to swipe it away, then get up and carry him with me downstairs. I put him in his high chair and give him a couple of toys to keep him entertained while I set up a pot of coffee and make his breakfast.

As I'm grabbing his oatmeal out of the microwave, I jump and look at my cell phone on the counter when it pings with a text. I might have been able to forget about Lex's mother's message after Blake's kiss, but once he and Maverick took off to take out the guests, it was right back to the front and center of my mind, and it's been there ever since.

The only thing that put me slightly at ease was that my dad explained to me last night that no judge would ever force visitation with a grandparent if it was not in the best interest of the child. And he also questioned whether Lex's parents really did retain a lawyer or whether they were just trying to scare me. From what he explained, most lawyers would not take on a case where they'd have a difficult time presenting it to a judge. And Lex's parents demanding grandparents' rights when their son is not on the birth certificate and has not requested a DNA test would really make things difficult.

"Mama!" Sam shouts, pulling me from my thoughts, and I smile at him.

"Food's coming, baby." I set down his bowl of oatmeal on the counter, then go to my cell phone and peek at the screen without touching it. I let out a breath when I see it's a text from Blake with a simple request that makes my heart beat a little differently.

Blake: Video call me when you're up. I want to see your and Sampson's faces.

I pick up my phone and press on his name, then touch the icon to call him, and the phone only rings once before he answers. "Hey, babe." He smiles, and Sampson, hearing his voice, starts chanting "Da, da, da," making him chuckle. "Let me talk to him, then I'll talk to you."

"Sure." I laugh, handing my phone over to Sampson; then I listen to him babble to Blake while I finish adding milk and butter to his oatmeal. By the time it's done and cool enough for him to eat, he's gone from talking to trying to devour my phone, so I take it from him and clean it off before looking at the screen.

"I wasn't sure you'd be up," he tells me.

"Sam is an early riser," I say, and just like yesterday, I see the ceiling of a room for a moment, then hear the whoosh of fabric and the sound of water turning on.

"He and I have that in common."

"He and I do *not* have that in common. He just left me no choice but to get with his program," I reply, and he comes back on-screen, grinning.

"Sorry, babe, I don't think that will change until he's a teenager. Then you'll be wishing he'd wake up to spend time with you."

"You're probably right about that," I agree, not really wanting to think about a time when my baby doesn't need me so much. "So how did it go last night?"

"All right, though I'm not sure Mav is going to be able to last the full four days. I might trade places with him tomorrow if he says he needs a break."

I try to hide the disappointment I'm feeling with a sympathetic smile. "Poor Maverick."

"The good news is Mason agreed to help run supplies the next few days, so you won't have to."

"That is good," I respond, because I really was not looking forward to driving the four-wheeler alone after only having one day of practice.

"The bad news is I won't be around, except to pick up meals and shit from the kitchen."

"Oh," I say quietly, and his expression softens.

"That said, I hope we're still on for this weekend."

"We're still on," I tell him softly, and he looks relieved.

"Good, and I'll call when I can, and if you can't get ahold of me, leave a message, and I'll get back to you as soon as I have a minute."

"Okay."

"Okay," he repeats. "Tell Sam I'll see him soon." With my throat tight, I nod. "Talk to you later, babe."

"Yeah, later." I hang up and look at Sam. "I'm in so much trouble, baby." I scoop him out a bite of his oatmeal and feed it to him. "So much trouble."

"I'd say so." My mom startles me, and I almost drop my phone. "Then again, it sounded to me like Blake is in just as much trouble as you are." She goes to the coffeepot and pours herself a cup. "How long have you two been seeing each other?"

"We haven't been seeing each other," I say, and she sends me a doubtful look. "Seriously, last weekend was the first time we spent any real time together, and yesterday—" I cut myself off.

"Yesterday what?"

"Nothing."

"Everly." Her tone and look let me know I need to start talking.

"Fine, he kissed me," I admit. I mean, it was just a peck on the lips. I shouldn't be embarrassed about that, right?

"He kissed you," she repeats, and I nod. "At work?"

"Yes."

"Everly, honey, I . . ." She comes over and takes a seat across from me. "I'm all for you finding someone, and I do like Blake, but I just . . . it's just . . ."

"He's my boss," I say, guessing that's what her issue is, because it's one of mine, and she nods. "I know. Believe me, it's something I've thought about."

"It's more than that, honey. I just want you to promise me that you will take your time and get to know him, really get to know him."

"I'm not rushing into anything. I learned what can happen when you do that, and I never want to go through that again, especially now that I have more than just myself to protect." I drop my eyes from hers. "Falling in love with the wrong person is not a mistake I ever want to repeat."

"You didn't do anything wrong." She frowns.

"Didn't I?" I frown back. "I jumped right into things with Lex without really finding out who he was, and I assumed we were on the same page, when the reality was we were in completely different books. I made a lot of mistakes when it comes to him."

"You fell in love." She reaches for my hand. "Do you know how many women fall in love, get married, and have kids, only to realize months, years, or even decades later that the person they chose wasn't who they thought they were?" Her hold on me tightens. "Now, I might not want you to jump into things with Blake or anyone else without getting to know them, but I also don't want you to have your walls up so high that you make it impossible for the right person to get to you."

She stands, letting my hand drop, then leans over and kisses my forehead, cupping my cheek as she meets my gaze. "Putting your heart on the line is scary, especially after getting hurt, but when you do find the right person, you will realize everything you went through was worth it. Every relationship is a learning experience. You find out what you need from someone and what you don't, what you like and dislike, and how you expect the person you chose to treat you."

She lets me go and kisses the top of Sam's head as tears fill my eyes. Mom continues, "Lex was a learning experience, and if you really think about it, he was one of the best things that happened to you, because at the end of the day, you wouldn't have had Sam without him."

With that statement hanging in the air, she picks up her coffee and walks across the kitchen to the doorway she came in through minutes ago, saying over her shoulder, "I'm going to get dressed."

"Mom," I call, and she stops to look at me. "I love you."

"I love you, too, honey." She gives me a soft look, then disappears out of sight.

Alone with Sam, I finish feeding him his breakfast while realizing my mom is right about one thing: without going through what I did with Lex, I wouldn't have the knowledge I do now, and most importantly, I wouldn't have Sam. And I don't even want to imagine my life without him. So maybe falling in love with Lex wasn't all bad.

~

I glance down at the GPS on my phone, then back at the road to confirm that I'm going the right direction. I make a left turn when the automated voice tells me to. It's Saturday, and after a week of video calls with Blake every morning, not seeing him at work every day, and random texts or short phone calls most evenings, I'm finally seeing him in person. Butterflies take flight in my stomach as we get closer to his house, while Sam starts to shout his dislike of being stuck in his car seat for more than ten minutes.

"We're almost there, baby." I turn on one of his favorite songs, which annoys me but thankfully distracts him. A few minutes later, the GPS announces I've reached my destination, and I just barely see a mailbox on the side of the road that's partially covered by the overgrowth of bushes. I turn down the one-lane dirt road after it and wonder if I'm going the right way as I continue to drive.

It isn't until Tutu comes running up to my car that I relax. Going around another curve, I have to blink at the house in front of me. The rock-covered monstrosity is huge and looks nothing like the house I imagined Blake would live in. I figured he would live in a log home like Tanner's or his parents', or maybe something cool and modern with lots of windows. I park next to a newer silver car in front of the closed garage, then shut down the engine and open my door. As soon as I get out, Tutu barks, bouncing on her back legs, her large size making it impossible for her to fully jump on me.

"Hey, girl." I laugh, scratching the top of her head, then tell her to sit so I can get Sam out of the back seat. Thankfully, she listens, but her body wiggles with excitement, letting me know just how hard it is for her to do so.

"Can I help you?" a woman asks, and I spin around to face her, holding my hand against my chest. She's older, with long dark-gray hair braided over her shoulder, weathered skin, and eyes so blue they look like crystals.

"Umm." I look around. "I'm here for Blake."

"Aww." She smiles. "I'm Tina. This is my place." She points to the house behind her. "Blake's house is a little farther up the road. We share a driveway."

"Oh, I'm sorry."

"It's not a big deal. It happens from time to time." She points across the hood of my car. "Just follow that road on the side of my garage up about a half mile, and you'll run smack-dab into his house."

"Okay, thanks." I open my door back up. "It was nice meeting you. I'm Everly, by the way."

"Nice meeting you, Everly." She lifts her hand and calls out to me before I close my door. "If you see my grandson, Edmond, on the way or find him hanging around Blake's house, I'd appreciate it if you'd tell him it's lunchtime, so he needs to come home and eat."

"I'll be sure to tell him." I laugh as I shut the door, then back up and drive around the side of her garage. I follow the road with Tutu chasing my car and barking, and a half mile or so later, the trees open up once more. A black house with an angular roof and large windows comes into view, the style 100 percent Blake, which makes me curious if he designed it himself. As I get closer, Blake steps out of the garage, followed closely by a boy around eight or nine who has the most gorgeous red hair I've ever seen in my life.

I park next to his truck and unhook my seat belt, and my heart does a double beat as he walks toward my car. I'm not sure if he got better looking since the last time I saw him, but the extra stubble on his jaw and his baseball cap, T-shirt, and loose shorts are definitely a good look on him.

"Hey," he says, opening my door and holding out his hand to help me out.

"Hey." I let out a long breath when he wraps his arms around me, and I melt into him. I didn't know how much I needed to be held until I was in his arms.

"I'm glad you're here."

"Me too," I say, and he leans back without letting me go and meets my gaze as I tip my head back. "I like your house."

"Thanks." He smiles softly, lifting his hand and using the tips of his fingers to swipe them across my forehead, his eyes watching them, then dropping to my lips. My stomach dances in anticipation when he tips his head down, and my toes curl as he brushes his lips across mine. The kiss is soft, barely a whisper, but it's still the second sweetest kiss I've ever received, the first being the last time he kissed me. I want to lean up on my tiptoes for more, but Sam starts to yell from his car seat, letting the world know he's not happy about being left out.

"I'd better get him." I laugh.

"I got him." He lets me go, then opens the back door, and I know the moment Sam sees Blake, because his cries of frustration turn into giggles of happiness. I smile, then look to my right and notice the little boy with red hair watching, with Tutu sitting at his side.

"Edmond?" I ask, and his head jerks back ever so slightly in surprise. "I met your grandma on the way here," I explain, and he relaxes. "I'm Everly."

"Are you Blake's girlfriend?"

I stare into his questioning eyes and try to figure out how to respond. I mean, I was just kissing Blake, and he is a kid, so I wouldn't feel right saying no, but I don't even know where Blake and I stand. So saying yes, especially with Blake close enough to hear me say the wrong thing, could be really awkward.

"Umm . . ."

"Yes, Ed, she's my girlfriend," Blake says easily as he emerges from the car with Sam, who looks so happy to be back with his friend.

"Cool." Edmond grins, then mutters, "I kinda guessed that when you kissed her."

"Right." Blake laughs, apparently not noticing me slightly freaking out about the fact that he just said we are together. Like *together* together. "Let's get your bike, bud. I'm sure your grandma is ready for you to be home." He heads into the garage with Sam on his hip, and I follow behind him with Edmond.

"She doesn't care," Edmond says, and there's something about the tone of his voice that hurts my heart.

"She asked me to tell you that lunch is ready," I tell him quietly. "If she's anything like my grandma was, that's code for she wants to spend time with you."

"Maybe." He shrugs, going to his bike, which is suspended upside down on two barrels in the middle of the garage.

"Take him for a minute, babe." Blake hands me Sam, and I kiss his cheeks to distract him as Blake helps Edmond put the chain back on his bike. When they finish, Blake takes his bike down, then flips it upright, and Edmond grabs hold of the handlebars and tosses his leg over the seat.

"Thanks," he tells him; then his eyes come to me and Sam. "Nice meeting you."

"You too, Edmond," I say softly, watching him roll out of the garage and head down the driveway, picking up speed as he goes. "He seems sweet."

"He's a good kid."

"Is there a story there?" I ask, turning to face him, and his expression gentles.

"His mom took off when he was a couple of months old, and his dad works on the pipelines, so he's not around much. Tina, his grandma, is doing what she can, but—"

"But he misses his dad," I say, cutting him off, and he nods. "Poor baby." My chest aches. I can only imagine what he must be feeling, especially being so young.

"He'll be okay. He has lots of people looking out for him." He rests his hand against my lower back, then asks, "Do you need to grab anything from your car before we head inside?"

"Sam's bag," I tell him, and before I can make a move to go get it, he walks out of the garage and grabs the bag from the back seat. When he comes back, he takes Sam from me, then motions for me to head for the stairs.

"I figured we could eat lunch here before we head out to the farm. Are you okay with that?" he asks, reaching around me to open the door.

"Yeah." I step inside a laundry-slash-mudroom that is, not surprisingly, super clean and organized, with all the shoes lined up perfectly on a stand near the door and cleaning supplies in baskets on the shelf. I slip off my boots when he kicks off his sneakers, then walk through the only door in the room that takes me right into a long, dark hallway.

"Head to the right."

I do, and soon we enter the kitchen, which is open to the living room. Even with the dark paint and furniture, the large windows offer lots of light, and the tall ceilings and open floor plan make the space feel bright and spacious.

"This is so cool." I look around. "It definitely screams you. Did you design it?"

"I did."

"I thought so." I take Sam's bag from him, set it on the counter, and dig through for his diapers, wipes, and changing pad. "I'm going to change him really quick, if you don't mind."

"Not at all." He hands Sam over to me. "While you do that, I'll start lunch. Are you good with roasted chicken, mozzarella, basil, and tomato panini sandwiches?"

"I'd be okay with peanut butter and jelly," I tell him truthfully. "But that also sounds delicious." I catch his smile as I leave the kitchen, and I carry Sam to the living room and lay him down on the couch on the pad. As always happens when I'm changing him, a wrestling match ensues. Despite how small he is, he's really fricking strong, so I'm a little worse for wear by the time I'm done.

As he waddles into the kitchen, I clean up the pillows that ended up on the floor, then grab his diaper and take it with me back to the kitchen, and Blake shows me where to toss it by opening one of the lower cabinets hiding the garbage cans.

"So tell me the latest with the ex," he says as I grab a small ball from Sam's diaper bag that makes a multitude of noises and give it to him to play with. Because I already opened up to him about what happened with Lex and the message I received from his mom, the question doesn't catch me off guard.

"It's been a quiet week." I sigh, leaning back against the counter next to where he's placing two buttery sandwiches into a metal contraption before closing the lid. "I haven't spoken to Lex since our last conversation or received a call from his parents' lawyer yet." I fiddle with the edge of my sweater. "Honestly, I wish that whatever was going to happen would just happen so I could deal with it and get it over with."

"Maybe your dad is right, and they haven't actually found a lawyer to take their case."

"Maybe," I agree as I take a seat on the floor with Sam so he can roll the ball to me. "How's your dad?"

"I don't know. He's been keeping shit to himself the last couple of weeks. Even when I ask about his treatments and what his doctors are saying, he's kept things vague."

"I'm sorry." I reach out and rest my hand against his thigh, and he meets my gaze as he covers my hand with his.

"Me too," he says, and the pain in his features makes my chest ache.

Licking my lips, I ask him gently, "Do you think it might be time to tell your mom and sister about what's going on?"

"It was time to tell them when he found out he had cancer." His jaw twitches, and I dig my fingers into his thigh. "I just . . . I don't . . . it's not my secret to tell."

"I get that, but they deserve to know, especially if—"

"Don't," he says, cutting me off, and even though he didn't raise his voice, it's clear I need to tread very carefully when talking about what might come of his father's diagnosis.

How no one has been able to see the pain he's been in from keeping this secret is astonishing to me. I saw it written all over his face in that photo on his grandmother's desk, and being around him the last few weeks, it's glaringly clear he's going through something difficult. Honestly, I'm angry with his dad for using his son's loyalty to him to keep a secret that's causing him pain, and I'm frustrated with his friends for not seeing that he's hurting.

"Okay," I say softly, and he gives my hand a squeeze. Then Sam comes over, probably feeling the strange energy, and reaches his arms out for Blake to pick him up. I stand, and my chest feels heavy as I watch Sam pat Blake's cheek, then rest his head against his shoulder.

"Thanks, big guy. I needed that," Blake tells him quietly, rocking him back and forth.

"You know I'm here if you need to talk about things," I remind him quietly when he meets my gaze, and his features soften, but he doesn't say anything. Then again, maybe he doesn't need to.

An hour later, with my stomach full from the delicious sandwich Blake made, I sit on his couch and laugh at Sam as he dances around the living room.

"I'd say he likes the movie," Blake says, and I turn to look at him and roll my eyes at the smug look on his handsome face.

"Don't gloat." I toss the pillow next to me at his head, and he catches it easily. When he finished making our lunch, he suggested putting on some movie about singing trolls for Sam while we ate, and I told him that he wouldn't be into it, because he's only ever really liked one TV program. Apparently, I was wrong, because Sam has been entertained for the last hour.

"So violent." He smiles. Then, when thunder sounds outside, he looks out the floor-to-ceiling window next to his fireplace, where his TV is hanging. "It's raining."

I follow his gaze and see fat drops of rain beating against the window.

"I didn't even think to check the forecast for today." I drag Sam onto my lap when he tries to crawl up onto the couch, and as soon as I have him in the crook of my arm, his head falls against my chest and his hand finds its way down the front of my shirt. "I think he's ready for a nap."

"Baba," Sam mumbles, and I slide my finger down his forehead and over his nose, the motion causing his eyes to slide half-closed.

"Do you want me to get his bottle?"

"Please," I say quietly, and he gets up, and I hear him moving around the kitchen. A moment later, he comes back and takes a seat next to me before passing the bottle over. As soon as it's in Sam's mouth, his eyes start to drift closed. "I think we'll have to plan a trip to the farm another day."

"It's not going anywhere." He touches Sam's hand, and I watch Sam's tiny fingers automatically wrap around his much larger one.

With Blake's weight leaning into me, and Sam against my chest mostly asleep, I can't help but wonder if this is what women who have children with men who care about them and their child feel every second of every day. Safe, supported, wanted. It's odd that I feel all those things with Blake, given that we're still getting to know each other, but then again, there's no denying that is exactly what I feel in this moment. And having it, I want it even more than I thought I did, only I really only want it with him.

Chapter 12

BLAKE

With Everly in the living room with Sampson, the two of them hanging on the couch and watching one of his shows, I place the potatoes I just finished wrapping in foil into the oven. Before Everly and Sam, the only time I was home was to sleep, and I never really cooked, even though it's something I love doing. As I slam the door closed, my cell across the kitchen beeps, letting me know I have a message. I grab it off the counter and read the text from my mom, asking if Everly and Sam are coming for dinner tomorrow. I text her back, letting her know I'll ask, then go to my message chain with Mav and scroll through my unanswered ones.

Yesterday, after Lauren and Oliver's group took off, he said he was going to head out of town for a couple of days, which is something we've all done after a rough trip. But him not returning any of my messages, along with how distracted he seemed, has me wondering if something else is going on with him.

"Why are you frowning at your phone?" Everly asks, coming into the kitchen, and I set down my cell, then reach for her hand.

"Nothing." I pull her over to stand in front of me, and she rests her hands against my chest, then looks into the living room to make sure Sam is okay.

"So you're just frowning to make sure you haven't forgotten how to?" she asks. I laugh, watching her smile. Damn, but I love her smile.

"No, just worried about Mav." I curl my hands around her waist, then slide them back to draw her closer. It feels good to be able to touch her, to be touched by her after fighting this for so long.

"Why?"

"He's not returning my messages," I tell her, and she tips her head to the side, looking concerned.

"Is that something he's done before?"

"No." I tuck a piece of hair that's fallen out of her ponytail behind her ear. "But he said he was heading out of town, so my guess is he just needs to decompress after Oliver and Lauren's group."

"Were they that bad?"

"Bad, no. Challenging, yes—especially with Jake acting like an entitled prick the entire time." Fuck, even saying his name causes that anger I felt when I found him cornering her in the hall to come flaring back to life.

"That guy was kind of a jerk." She bites her bottom lip. "Should you go see if you can find him just to make sure he's okay?"

"If Mav doesn't want to be found, no one is finding him." I slide one hand up her back. "I'm sure he's fine."

"Okay." She doesn't look convinced, so I decide it's time to change the subject to take her mind off it.

"My mom wants to know if you and Sam are coming to dinner tomorrow."

"Oh." Her eyes scan my face, and I can see the wheels in her head turning. "I . . . well . . ." She licks her lips, then tries to take a step away from me, but I hold steady.

"Well, what?"

"We need to talk."

"All right." I lean back against the counter, bringing her with me. "Let's talk."

"I think it would be easier to talk to you if you weren't holding me." She laughs nervously.

"And I think it will be easier to listen if you're right here."

"Fine." She sighs when she sees I'm not going to let her go. "I want . . ." She licks her lips. "No, I *need* to know where we stand," she says, and my brows draw together. "Don't frown at me."

"I'm trying to figure out what you mean by *where we stand*."

"I mean, are we together? Are we just seeing each other? Or are we, like . . . seeing each other but also dating other people?"

"Fuck no to the last, and yes to the first," I bite out, and she pats my chest.

"Don't growl. It's just a question. I need to make sure we're on the same page." She leans over to pick up Sam when he comes over to where we're standing, and I wrap my arms around both of them. "I also want to make sure you realize that dating me means you're dating him, so—"

"Babe," I say, cutting her off with a squeeze. "I know what I'm getting myself into, so I don't need you to prepare me for that. And if I did have any concerns about dating a woman with a child, I wouldn't even attempt to go there."

"Okay, good," she says quietly.

"Anything else?" I ask when she looks like she wants to say more.

"There is also the matter of you being my boss."

"Right." I take Sam from her when he reaches for me but still keep hold of her. "Your job will never be in jeopardy, and not just because Mav and Tanner would kick my ass, but because I wouldn't do that to you."

"But if this doesn't work"—she shakes her head—"I would have to quit. I couldn't—"

"Being with you feels right," I say, interrupting again before she can finish, because no way do I want to even think about this ending up any other way but with us together. "I haven't felt this content since . . ." Fuck, never. I've *never* felt this. "I don't know that I've ever felt this content. I want this to work. I want more days just like this with you and Sam, and if by some chance things between us don't work, we'll figure it out. Okay?"

"Okay," she agrees, visibly relaxing, and Sam wraps his arm around her neck while keeping hold of me.

"Now kiss me and let me finish getting dinner ready. I don't want you and Sam driving home too late." With her expression soft, she starts to lean around Sam but stops when he squeals and lunges between us, slobbering on her cheek and mine.

"All right, mister." She laughs, taking him from me and placing him on her hip. "Let's let Blake finish cooking for us." She maneuvers him so that she can kiss me, then carries him to the living room. With the two of them a room away, I broil salmon steaks and steam some broccoli, realizing that only because the two of them are here does my house actually feel like a home.

~

"Okay, I didn't want to say anything before, but it's seriously weird how much Sampson looks like you when you were little," Margret says, her attention focused on Taylor and Sampson, who are playing with a pile of blocks Dad dumped in the middle of the living room for them to play with.

"I was thinking the same thing," Mom whispers, glancing over at the recliner where Everly's curled up, watching the kids play.

"Right? The two of them could totally be twins." Margret doesn't whisper, and I shake my head at my sister. "What? I love this for you. It's about darn time you realize work isn't everything."

"What's going on?" my dad asks, joining us at the island in the kitchen, and like earlier when we arrived for dinner, I can't help but notice the dark circles under his eyes and how exhausted he looks.

"We were just saying how much Sampson looks like Blake when he was little," Mom says, and Dad leans into her with his hand on her back.

"He really does." He meets my gaze, smiling.

"How's your headache?" Mom asks him quietly, and he kisses her cheek.

"Getting better."

"I really wish you would go to the doctor and see why you keep getting them."

"You worry too much. I'm fine," he tells her gently, then heads into the living room to take a seat on the floor where the kids are.

I glance at my mom and Margret, catching the worried look the two of them share, then look into the living room and find Everly biting her lip while watching my dad play with Taylor and Sam. My stomach churns, and my hands ball into fists. I want to scream. I want to rage and demand that he be honest, but I can't, because I promised I would keep his secret.

At first, I understood. I understood he didn't know what would come of his diagnosis and that he didn't want to worry anyone. I understood him wanting to keep his family from unnecessary pain. But now . . . now, it feels like I'm an accomplice in a lie that will eventually lead to my mother and sister resenting me, because the option to come to terms with things is being taken away from them without them even knowing it.

"Are you okay, honey?" Mom's hand lands on mine, and I curl my fingers around hers and force myself to relax.

"Yeah." I meet her gaze, and she eyes me doubtfully.

"You know, with no guests coming in for another week, we should all go to Bigfork," she says, referring to my family's property on Flathead Lake. The house we own there is over six thousand square feet, with a huge kitchen, living room, heated pool, and direct access to the lake. Every year when Margret and I were growing up, that was where we spent our summer breaks, and as we've gotten older, we've made a point to spend at least a couple of weekends there as a family when we can all get time off. "Everly and Sam would love it, and I'll watch Sam so you and Everly can spend some time alone." She squeezes my fingers. "It would be good for you to take a little break and get away."

"I don't—"

"It would be good for your dad too," Mom says, cutting me off. "He's been under a lot of pressure with work. He hasn't even been able to take his plane out recently." His job as the CEO of a log-home business is stressful at times, but that's not what is stressing him out right now.

"I love this idea," Margret says, grabbing her phone. "I'll send Ben a message. He owes me some time off, so I'm sure he won't mind."

"Before you do that, I need to talk to Everly and see if it's something she wants to do," I tell her, and she rolls her eyes, then looks into the living room and calls out Everly's name.

"Yeah?" Everly answers, and Margret motions for her to come into the kitchen, so she gets up. When she's close, I take her hand and pull her to stand between my spread thighs.

"Awww, how cute are you two?" Margret sighs dramatically, and Everly shakes her head at her while her cheeks get a little darker.

"So what's going on?" She looks between us.

"Mom just suggested that we take a few days off and head to our family's house on Flathead Lake."

"Okay, cool, just let me know what I need to do while you're gone."

"Babe." I smile. "I'd want you and Sam to come with us. I just need to know if you think you can do that."

"Umm." She locks her gaze with me and asks quietly, "Really?"

"Really," I say just as quietly.

"Well, you are my boss." She smiles saucily. "So if you say I can go, then I guess I can go."

"Right." I grin, and she giggles. Fuck, but I love her laugh.

"All right." She rests her hand on my shoulder. "But what about work? We don't have clients coming in this week, but we do have clients coming in—"

"Please don't start acting like Blake," Margret groans. "Especially when Blake isn't even acting like Blake. We have internet and a telephone at the house, so if either of you really feel like you need to do some work, you can do it from the lake."

"Well, then, it's a yes from me," Everly says, and my mom beams while Margret tosses her hands in the air and wiggles around.

"What are we celebrating?" Dad asks, coming over. He's holding both kids, and he passes Taylor to Margret and Sam to Everly.

"We're going to the lake house," Mom tells him with a wide smile, and he looks around at all of us.

"I'd like that," Dad says quietly, resting his hand on my shoulder and squeezing it once before going to Mom and wrapping his arms around her. "We could all use a little time away from everything. Maybe I'll see if Grandma can come."

"Definitely, that would be awesome," Margret chirps, and Everly nods. Sam shouts, "Da, da," while lunging for me.

"Then it's settled," Mom says, and I nod my agreement.

It's settled; I just really hope all of us being in the same house for more than a day doesn't end up blowing up in our faces. It's going to be a lot more difficult for my dad to keep his secret, and if the truth does come out, he won't be the only one answering some really fucking uncomfortable questions.

Chapter 13

EVERLY

"I just don't know what I'm going to do with myself all day without Sam here to keep me company." My mom pouts as I grab a stack of T-shirts out of my dresser and take them to the bed, where my suitcase is.

"You'll be fine." I place them inside the bag, then go to the closet to get some jeans and a couple of sweaters. "I mean, you did have a life before Sam and I moved in with you."

"Yeah, but it was a boring life," she says, and I poke my head out of the closet and look at where she's sitting on the bed, holding Sam.

"You can always help Dad in the office for a couple of days, since Blake's grandma is supposed to come up for a night or two while we're there."

"Do you want me and your father to get divorced?" she asks, and I laugh as I grab a couple of pairs of jeans off a hanger, along with two of my favorite lounge sweaters.

"All right, then maybe you can finally go take that hot yoga class you were telling me about."

"I'm not in the mood to be sweaty."

"What about the book you were saying you wanted to read a few weeks ago?"

"Too many words."

"Well, then I don't know what you're going to do while we're gone."
I laugh.

"Me neither." She hugs Sam. "Are you sure you don't just want to
leave him with me while you go on your trip?"

"I don't think either he or I would do very well being away from
each other that long."

"I guess you're right," she agrees as I toss some panties and a few
bras into the bag. "I know! I can come with you guys."

"Mom." I roll my eyes at her. "What would Dad do without you
while you were gone?"

"I don't know. That seems like a him problem, not a me problem,"
she says.

"Right." I laugh and then pick up my phone when it starts to ring.
I answer, still chuckling at my mom. "Hello?"

"Hello, this is Lucas with Greenburn Family Law. I'm calling to
speak with Everly Standler," a man says, and my laughter dies a quick
death as my stomach drops.

"This is Everly."

I wrap an arm around my middle while my mom mouths, "Who
is it?"

"Hi, Everly, do you have a moment to talk?" Lucas asks.

"I do," I say, and Mom starts shaking her head frantically while
flailing her arms about. "Sorry, can you hold for one second?"

"Sure," he says, and I put the call on mute.

"Who is it?" Mom asks, and I swallow.

"It's a family law lawyer," I tell her, and her expression becomes
concerned before she stands suddenly.

"Okay, it's okay. Let's go downstairs." She leaves the room, still
holding Sam and talking over her shoulder. "When we get there, you're
going to put the call on speaker, and I'm going to record it so your
father can hear exactly what is said."

"That's smart." I follow her into the kitchen, where she grabs her phone off the counter, then presses record and motions for me to unmute the call.

"Sorry about that. I'm here," I tell Lucas.

"It's okay," he says. "As I was saying, I work with Greenburn Family Law, and I'm representing Ginny and Jeff Thines."

"Okay," I say when he doesn't add more.

"They would like to talk to you about working out a visitation agreement with their grandson, Sampson Thines."

"Standler."

"Pardon?"

"My son's last name is Standler, not Thines. That's what it says on his birth certificate."

"I see." He clears his throat. "I'm contacting you today to see if we can set up mediation between you and Mr. and Mrs. Thines in my office."

"Did Ginny tell you that I did meet with them, and that the first thing she did was demand I get a DNA test for my son?"

"She mentioned that unfortunate situation when we spoke," he says, sounding genuinely sympathetic. "These situations can be tricky, especially when emotions are running so high."

"Lucas, this situation was not tricky until I was accused of lying about who Sam's father is, which is laughable, given that I have not asked his father to help support his child since birth." I take a breath to get my temper under control so I don't say something I will regret. "I don't know if you're a parent, but if you are, I know you would never put your child in a situation with people who could treat them poorly. And after the way Ginny acted, I'm not exactly comfortable having my son around her."

"That is completely understandable." He again sounds genuine. "And Ginny did express her regret for the way she acted."

"Right," I mumble, not sure I believe him, since she didn't ever tell me that she was sorry. In fact, the only time I heard from her was when she said I should be prepared to hear from a lawyer.

"I believe that if you agree with mediation, it will help."

"You're representing them. You're not exactly a neutral party," I say, pointing out the obvious.

"If you're more comfortable, I can have a counselor that we work with from time to time sit in on the meeting," he says, and I sigh.

"I'm going to need some time to think about this, Lucas."

"That's completely understandable."

"I'm going out of town for a few days. I'll call and let you know my decision when I get back."

"I look forward to hearing from you then," he says, and I hang up the call while my mom stops recording.

"Well, I'm proud of you for standing your ground," she remarks, and I let out a long breath, then look at where Sam has wandered into the living room to play with his toys. "What do you think you're going to do?"

"I think . . ." I rub my forehead. "I don't know. Part of me wants to say no and fight them until they give up, but another part of me doesn't want Sam to come to me in fifteen or twenty years and ask why I didn't let him see his grandparents."

"I can understand that," Mom says softly, and I take a seat at the kitchen table.

"What would you do?"

"I don't know, honey. I really don't know. It's not a normal situation. I know that if I were in their shoes, I would want the chance to get to know Sam, but I also know I would never have acted the way Ginny did, even if I did have doubts."

"Yeah, and that's what worries me. What if she acts like that again or says something to Sam when he's old enough to understand?"

She takes my hand. "First, you won't know what will happen unless you decide to meet with them. Second, you don't have to decide anything right now. Take the time while you're away to think and pray about it. And know that your father and I will support you in whatever you want to do."

"Thanks, Mom."

"Anytime." She lets my hand go. "Now, you need to get back upstairs to finish packing while I spend some time with my grandson."

I glance at the clock and see that Blake is going to be here in less than thirty minutes, which means I need to get moving. "I shouldn't be much longer." I stand.

"Take your time. You know it's not a burden for me to spend time with my favorite guy," she says, and I bend to kiss her cheek, then head upstairs.

When I get to my room, I get back to packing while thinking about the phone call with Lucas and what my mom said. Not surprisingly, I don't come up with an answer to what I should do by the time the doorbell rings, letting me know Blake is here.

"Hey," I hear my mom say as I roll my suitcase to the edge of the stairs; then Sam squeals in happiness. With a smile on my face, I start to pull my bag down the steps behind me, listening to the *thump, thump, thump* as I go.

"Are you moving into the lake house?" Blake asks, and I turn to find him coming up the steps toward me, looking as handsome as ever in a thermal the color of his eyes with a ball cap on his head and jeans that fit him way too well.

"Maybe." I shrug, and he smiles before touching his lips to mine and taking the handle from me.

"I got this."

"Thanks," I say to his back as he carries the bag easily down the stairs. When we reach the bottom, I shake my head at my mom, who has tears in her eyes as she holds on to Sam for dear life, even though he's clearly attempting to get to Blake. "I know you are not crying."

"I can't help it." She pops out her bottom lip. "I'm going to miss him."

"We'll be back in just a few days," I assure her with a hug.

"I know." She hugs me back, then looks at Blake. "You'd better take care of my babies."

"I promise," he assures her, taking Sampson when she finally gives him up; then he tips his head down to me. "Do you have everything?"

"I think so. I didn't pack much food stuff for Sam, since I figured there was probably a store close to the house that we could stop at to get him what he likes."

"There's a store close." He reaches out to give my hand a squeeze, then slides his fingers through mine. How I can feel connected to one person after such a short time is anyone's guess, but there's no denying the connection I feel to the man at my side holding my son.

"Then I guess we're ready," I tell him, and he lets my hand go so he can take the suitcase, but Mom stops him by grabbing the handle.

"I'll help you guys out." She opens the door with a smile, and Blake grabs Sam's travel crib, which is propped up next to the door.

When we get to the truck, he hands Sam off to Mom so he can put our stuff in the bed of the truck, then waits until she's finished loving on him before putting him in his seat. After another long hug from my mom, I get into my seat, buckle in, and wait while my mom and Blake talk before he joins me.

"Is everything okay?" I ask when he gets in behind the wheel, and he turns to me with a smile on his face.

"She was just making sure I understood how important it is that you and Sam get back here in one piece." He puts on his seat belt, then starts the engine.

"What part of you did she threaten to cut off if that didn't happen?" I ask, and he grimaces. "If it makes you feel any better"—I pat his thigh—"she hates blood and would probably throw up and pass out before causing any real harm."

"Good to know," he mutters, making me laugh as he pulls away from my parents' house.

~

With Sam finally asleep, I carry him over to the travel crib set up in my room and carefully lay him down, then pat his bottom when he rolls to his stomach. Once I know he's fully back to sleep, I place his blanket over him, then grab the baby monitor and a sweater before I head for the sliding door that leads to the deck outside my room.

When we arrived earlier today at Blake's family's house, while Margret, Janet, and I were making a shopping list, I learned that Janet and Dave both designed the house not long after they got married, before Janet gave birth to Blake and Margret, while Dave was working as an architect. They thought at the time that it would be the home they would raise their kids in. They had no idea Dave's business would expand and grow, and they would eventually move. Even now, you can feel how much love was put into the house and that they wanted it to feel like a place you'd want to come home to. Heck, I would want to live here now.

When I get outside, I walk past Blake's room, next to mine, and find it dark inside, which means he's probably still in the kitchen with his mom. His dad went to lie down not long after dinner, and Margret went to put Taylor to bed around the same time I put Sam to sleep.

I go to the large double doors off the kitchen and peek inside, seeing Blake, his mom, and his sister sitting in the kitchen, talking. I decide to give them some time alone. I know Janet and Margret might not be aware of Dave's diagnosis, but that doesn't mean they don't know something is going on with him. You can see it when they look at him and feel it in the air when he's around. They're worried, and not knowing is probably making it worse.

Honestly, I'm worried that when the truth does come out, it's going to be difficult for Margret and Janet to understand why Dave didn't want to tell them the truth, and they might end up resenting him. With a sigh, I set Sam's monitor down on one of the tables near the firepit and take a seat.

I prop my feet up on the edge of the deck and watch the sky turn cotton candy pink, blue, and purple over the lake as I wrap my sweater around me. One thing for sure is it's beautiful out here, especially with the way the house is built near the edge of a rocky cliff, making it seem from up here like you're floating on top of the water.

"Do you want me to start a fire?" Blake asks behind me, and I meet his gaze over my shoulder.

"If you want." I watch him get closer, and my belly warms from the look of contentment on his face. It's good to see him relaxed and happy.

"Fire it is." He bends to kiss me, then pulls back just an inch. "Sam get to sleep okay?"

"Yeah, he's normally really good about going to sleep, and he had a big day, so he was tired."

"Good." He kisses me once more, then stands and heads across the deck. He flips a switch on the wall before coming back to the firepit and opening a door on it, where he does something I can't see. But a second later, flames burst to life. "Mom and Margret are downstairs watching a movie. They didn't even ask if we wanted to join them," he says, taking a seat next to me.

"That was rude," I mumble, and he grins while placing my legs over his.

"Right? I thought so too."

Relaxing against him, I rest my head on his shoulder and my arm across his waist. "I think I really might move here."

"Am I invited?"

"I don't know. What can you bring to the table?"

"Not much," he says quietly, and my chest feels funny, because I feel like he thinks that's true.

"You're handsome."

"Looks fade," he replies easily, smoothing his hand up and down my arm.

"You can cook," I try again.

"So can a lot of people."

"You're kind."

"I don't know about that," he says, and I turn to face him, then straddle his lap, placing my hands against his chest.

"You're one of the best men I know, Blake. You're dependable, which is why your friends and family know they can count on you. You're generous, smart . . . and funny at times."

"Just at times?" he jokes, grabbing hold of my hips.

"I'm being serious right now," I say firmly, and his expression softens. "Under all your sharp edges, you're soft, a safe place to fall. A safe place for Sam, for your mom, your sister, your friends, your dad, and even Edmond and his grandma. The good thing about all your sharp edges is that when you let someone past them, they are safe, maybe safer than they were before."

"Fuck, Everly," he hisses like he's in pain.

"You've become my safe place," I tell him honestly, and I watch his jaw tighten. "The thing is, I would like to be that for you too."

"I don't want you to be my safe place." The statement cuts through me, causing pain, and I try to move, but he holds me firmly in place. "Since meeting you, I've felt more alive than I have in years." He moves his hands to my neck and slides them up to cup my face, his thumbs gliding over my cheeks. "I don't know why I was working so hard at avoiding life, but the truth is, I was. Then you came along and showed me what I was missing." I swallow hard as tears fill my eyes, then drop my forehead down to rest against his. "You and Sam have brought me back to life."

"I think I'm going to cry."

"Please don't. I don't think I can handle seeing you cry."

"They would be happy tears," I point out, and he digs his fingers into my scalp, then kisses me. This kiss starts like the others we've shared; then his teeth nip my bottom lip. I open on a gasp, then whimper when his tongue slides across mine.

Using his hand in my hair, he tips my head to the side and deepens the kiss. The space between my legs floods with heat, and my nipples pebble against the lace of my bra, making me more aware than I have ever been of just how sensitive they are. He hardens between my legs, and I moan into his mouth as he groans, grabbing my ass with one hand and using it to pull me more firmly against him.

"Oh, Blake," I pant when his mouth leaves mine, and he kisses and nips my jaw, then down my neck. I hold on to him for dear life as his mouth comes into contact with the tops of my breasts, and I swear I might just come apart from the friction between us.

I thought I knew what it was like to be turned on. I thought I knew what lust felt like. But having this here and now, I realize I didn't know anything.

"Fuck, I want to touch you." His hot breath dances across my skin while his fingers dig into my ass. "I want to shove my hand down the front of your pants and see exactly how wet you are for me, what you taste like." He licks the top of my breast. "What you look like." He lifts his hips, and his length rubs across my clit, making me cry out.

"Blake, I need you."

"I know." He leans me forward and grabs the monitor off the table, then stands, keeping hold of me. I wrap my legs around his hips as he walks across the deck, then nip his neck when he slides the door to his room open. Like mine, there isn't much in the room except a bed and a dresser.

He shuts the door and places me on my feet so he can walk around the bed and flip on the lamp. Soft light fills the room, and I lick my lips as nervousness fills my stomach. I don't have a lot of time to over-think how shy I'm suddenly feeling, because he whips the long-sleeved thermal he's wearing over his head and tosses it to the floor. I study his muscular torso, the tattoos on his arm and side of his chest and the deep V of his waist as he walks back toward me.

His hand reaches out to me, and I know he's giving me a choice. I can take it, or I can walk away. My hand rises, and when his fingers lock around mine, he pulls me a step closer. "You okay?"

"Yes," I breathe; then his mouth lands on mine and his hands rid me of my sweater before they move up my sides, taking my shirt up with them as they go. I lose him for a brief moment as he pulls my shirt off, then curl my hands around his waist as he unhooks my bra and slides it from my shoulders. I let it fall to the floor, then tip my head back as his lips and teeth work their way down my neck to my breast, and he moves me to the bed, easing me down onto the soft surface.

His fingers curl into the edge of my pants and panties; then in one smooth move, he rips them off, tossing them behind him carelessly. With his hands on my thighs, he spreads my legs, then places one knee on the bed, then the other. When his weight settles on top of me, I wrap my leg around his hips and moan when he captures one of my nipples and tugs while he cups my free breast in his hand.

The zing of pleasure that zips through me catches me off guard, and I dig my nails into his biceps. When he captures my mouth, I want to beg him to go back to what he was doing; then his hand skates down my stomach, and his fingers dive between the lips of my sex.

He finds my swollen clit with ease, and my back arches off the bed as I cry out his name. "Blake."

"So wet." He bites his lip, leaning back, his eyes wandering over my body that's spread out for him, his fingers still working me over. When he gets his fill, his head drops, and he pulls my nipple into his mouth once more, sucking deep before traveling his lips down my stomach. His big hands hold my thighs open wide so he can bury his face between my legs.

Not sure if I should push him away or latch onto him to keep him in place, I grab onto the top blanket on the bed and hold on for dear life. Licking, nipping, sucking, his mouth works me over, and just when I think it can't get any better, his fingers fill me up. I fly over the edge when they pump against that hidden spot inside me.

Darkness engulfs my vision as I fall, my body spasming, my core contracting, as I come harder than I have in my life.

"So sweet," he whispers, kissing my thigh, then stomach, before moving back. I open my eyes, still panting, and watch him grab a foil packet from his pocket, then take off his jeans. The sight of him, of all of him, is almost too much for my mind to take in. He's really beautiful *everywhere.*

As he gets back on the bed and uses his teeth to rip open the gold packet, my stomach dances with anticipation, and I don't hesitate to open myself up to him once more. Now more than ever, I want to feel him, all of him. I want to connect with him, be connected *to* him. As he slides the condom down his length, I wrap my other hand around his and help, then lean up to kiss him.

His body comes down on top of mine, his heavy weight making me feel small. I pull back to look at him as I line him up with my entrance. The look in his eyes makes me feel powerful. I've never had a man look at me like he does. Like I have the ability to shut off the world or light it up. It's a heady sensation.

As he begins to slide inside me, I bite my lip. He's so thick it's almost painful. "So damn tight," he groans, dropping his forehead to mine. "Fuck, you feel good . . . hot . . . wet."

"More." I lift my hips, listening to him bite back a curse as he slides even deeper. My neck arches, and my toes curl. I've never felt so full before. "Oh God," I breathe when he slides out, then back in even deeper than before.

"You're killing me, baby. I wanna fuck you so hard."

"Do it."

"I can't." He bites my chin, then my earlobe. "People are here, and Sam's asleep. If I fuck you like I really want, I'm sending the bed through the wall."

"Oh," I moan, wrapping my legs tighter around his hips as he fucks me slow, so deep. He might want to fuck me hard, but the way he's doing it is sending me closer and closer to the edge of something I know is going to be overwhelming.

My body starts to burn up from the inside out as his hands move over my body and mine over his. Our mouths battle in a messy duel, neither of us caring as we climb higher and higher together. Just when I think I know I'm going to combust, his thrusts speed up, and my fingers dig into his ass, holding on tight.

"Everly." His hips jerk, and mine follow suit as his name spills from my lips on a silent cry. I jump with him over the edge, and then we both fly higher and higher until nothing but he and I exist. We both might have been lost, but I know in that moment that we have ourselves and each other. I just pray that what we have built is strong enough to withstand what might come.

Chapter 14

EVERLY

"Up, up, up, da, da!" Sampson shouts, waking me, and I blink my eyes open, finding the room lit with early-morning light. I start to sit up before a warm, heavy weight lands on my stomach, stopping me before I can.

"I got him." Blake looms over me, and his fingers touch my chin as his eyes search mine, and he smiles. Gah, I love his smile. "Good morning."

"Good morning," I whisper, feeling a little off kilter waking up with him, and his smile turns into a grin before he leans in and places a soft kiss on my lips, causing a tingle to spread down my spine.

"You okay?"

I bite my lip as I think about his question. Honestly, last night was amazing, completely unexpected, but so completely right. I knew us sharing what we did would change things between us. I just had no idea how connected I would feel to him now.

Instead of saying all that and maybe looking crazy, I nod. "Yeah."

"Good." He kisses my forehead, and my heart feels funny in my chest as I watch him get up and put on a T-shirt that was hanging over the bottom edge of the bed before going to where Sam is standing with his arms above his head. When he picks him up and kisses his cheek, he whispers something I can't hear, and my nose stings.

What might be a throwaway moment to most is so fricking huge to me, and as much as I love it, I'm honestly scared to death I'm going to get used to this and it's going to be taken away. So I'm stuck in this strange place where I want to put everything on the line, while at the same time I want to protect myself and my son from getting hurt.

"Mama," Sam says, and I focus on my boy as Blake sets him down on the end of the bed, and he stumbles his way to me.

"Morning, baby." I wrap my arms around him and kiss his cheek as I rock him back and forth. "Are you hungry?"

"Baba."

"No bottle." I tickle him when he pops out his bottom lip. "But you can have some milk in a cup."

"Mwilk," he repeats, then looks at Blake. "Mwilk, banna."

"I think we can make that happen." Blake picks him up, and I toss back the blanket, then dig through my suitcase for a bra and maneuver it on under my tank, then grab a sweatshirt and pull it on.

"I need to use the restroom and brush my teeth."

"Go first, then I'll go after you," he says, carrying Sam over to the balcony door so he can look outside.

"Are you sure?"

"Yeah." He sends me a soft look right before I head out of the bedroom and across the hall. I quickly go through my morning routine, then trade places with him. When he comes back, we head toward the kitchen hand in hand. The closer we get, the more it becomes clear that someone has been busy. It smells like the best kind of breakfast—bacon and pancakes.

"Good morning," Dave greets us, his eyes dropping to our hands. "How'd you two sleep?"

"Great." I feel my cheeks get warm, even though I'm pretty sure no one could hear us last night, with our rooms on the opposite side of the house from everyone else's. But you never know.

"I hope you guys are hungry." Janet comes out of the pantry, holding up a container of syrup, before she turns to face the stove, and I wonder if it's just me or if she looks like she was crying. "I got a little carried away." She keeps her head slightly down as Blake walks over to kiss her cheek.

"Sam and I are hungry," Blake tells her, wrapping his arm around her shoulder and keeping Sam on his hip while I take a seat on the stool next to Dave. "You okay, Mom?"

"I just didn't sleep great." She tips her head back to look up at him and pats his cheek. "My hip was just annoying me last night."

"You need to finally talk to your doctor about it," Dave tells her, and she looks at him, something about her expression putting me on edge.

"Do I?" she asks him sarcastically.

"It would be smart; you don't want it to get worse."

"No, I guess we don't want that now, do we?" Her smile is off, and Blake's brows drag together while Dave seems to stiffen ever so slightly.

"Good morning, family," Margret sings, cutting through the weird vibe in the room as she follows Taylor into the kitchen with a smile on her face. "How did everyone sleep?" She kisses her dad's cheek while Taylor goes over to her grandma for her to pick her up.

I meet Blake's gaze when I feel him looking at me and shrug when he gives me a *what the fuck* look, because I don't know what's going on or what happened.

"Did you two lovebirds have a good night?" Margret asks, bumping into her brother with a saucy smile pointed in my direction, and I shake my head, watching her laugh.

"Leave your brother and Everly alone and get plates down so we can eat," Janet orders, carrying Taylor to Dave, who places her on his lap and hands her a piece of bacon off a plate in the middle of the counter.

"You're no fun." Margret sighs, and Janet rolls her eyes at her daughter.

141

"Can I help with anything?" I ask.

"You can pour coffee for everyone," Janet tells me, and I get up and walk around the island into the kitchen, pausing when Blake stops me to kiss my temple, which makes Margret sigh dreamily this time.

"You should take Everly out in one of the canoes today, and I'll watch Sam for you two," Janet says as I begin to pour coffee into the mugs I pulled down from the cabinet, and I glance over my shoulder at Blake.

"Everly doesn't really love outdoorsy stuff."

"You'll love it," Janet tells me as I finish off the last of the coffee. "There's nothing better than being out in the middle of the lake, surrounded by quiet."

"I don't know."

"It'll be fun," Blake assures me with a smile.

"All right." I give in, hoping I don't regret it.

～

"It's pretty out here." I carefully glance around, my life jacket and my grip on the canoe preventing me from moving too much.

"I'd be more inclined to believe you, baby, if your knuckles weren't turning white from holding on so tight." Blake laughs, and I scrunch my nose at him.

"I felt the water. It's not exactly warm, and I have no desire to end up in the lake."

"You're not going to end up in the lake." He shakes his head at me as he rows us toward a small tree-covered island.

"Whatever," I mutter, then look over his shoulder at the house, which is getting farther away. I see Sam and Janet on the top balcony with Margret and Taylor, with Dave nowhere in sight. "Do you think your mom knows about your dad?" I ask quietly.

"I don't know." His shoulders rise as he inhales a deep breath. "If she doesn't know for sure, I think she suspects something is going on."

"It's difficult not to when he's visibly lethargic."

"There's that," he agrees and then stops rowing. "What would you do? Would you tell your mom if it was your dad asking you to keep his secret?"

"I want to say that I would, but honestly I don't know if I would be strong enough to hurt my mom like that, or my dad."

"Yeah," he says before he starts to row once more. Then he adds quietly, "My dad took me off his contact list with his doctor."

"What do you mean?"

"His doctor can no longer legally give me any information about my father." His jaw twitches. "I called him yesterday before I came to pick you up, hoping he would give me an update, but he told me that he could no longer share my dad's information with me."

"Why would your dad do that?"

"My guess?" he asks, and I nod, even though I'm pretty sure I already know the reasons why. "He's now trying to protect *me*."

I bite my inner cheek as my nose stings, and tears fill my eyes. I hate the idea of what that means for Dave and his family. I *really* hate what that might mean for Blake. "I'm sorry, honey."

"Me too." His expression gentles, and he leans across the space between us to wipe away the wetness from my cheeks. "No crying."

"I'm not doing it on purpose."

"I know you're not." He leans back and looks around. "Have you ever heard of the Flathead Lake Monster?"

"The what?" I wipe my face with the sleeve of my shirt and go along with him changing the subject, because he obviously doesn't want to talk about his dad anymore.

"The Flathead Lake Monster, like the Loch Ness Monster, only here in Montana."

"That's not a real thing." I roll my eyes at him.

"It is. The Kootenai tribe was said to live on an island in the middle of the lake, and one winter when they were changing camps, the lake was frozen over, so they decided to cross it. Two girls saw what they thought were large antlers sticking out of the ice and decided to cut them off. As they started to chop away at the ice to get to them, the monster's head appeared, and then he shook, causing the ice on the lake to break up. It's said they used magic to get away, but some of the tribe drowned."

"You're serious?"

"There's been other reports since then, some even recently," he says, and I look around, feeling totally freaked out, because I do believe that a lot of Native American folklore comes from pieces of truth.

"Have you ever seen anything out here?"

"No, but one summer when Margret and I were probably eleven or twelve, we spent the entire month we were here trying to catch him. We set up traps and hidden cameras, but we never got any proof that he exists."

"I bet that was a letdown."

"Yeah, we had big plans for all the money we thought we'd make off the pictures." He smiles as I laugh.

"What was the biggest thing you were going to buy with the money?"

"A speedboat, or at least that's what I wanted. I don't remember what Margret wanted." He shrugs.

"Poor kid." I pout for eleven-year-old him, watching him laugh, then scream when something jumps out of the water on my right side. Like any sane person, I dodge to the left to avoid getting eaten by what I'm sure is the lake monster, and the canoe goes with me. When it rocks under my weight, I fly back to the right and latch onto the edge of the boat right before it rolls to the side.

Cold water smacks me in the face as I fall into the lake, and I hear Blake shout my name right before I go under. With my life vest on, I'm not submerged for more than a second before I pop back up. I knock my head on something hard and start sputtering. Kicking my feet, I look around and scream "Blake!" at the top of my lungs.

"I'm here." He spins me around to face him in the water, his eyes wandering over my face. "Are you okay?"

"Yeah, yeah, fine."

"You're bleeding." He touches my hairline, and I do the same and look at my fingers, tinged with pink water. "It's not a big cut, just a scrape. You're okay."

"Do you think the monster can smell blood?" I latch onto him and attempt to look at the water below us, which is not clear enough to see through.

"There's no monster, Everly."

"You're the one who told me about the monster," I cry. "You can't tell me it's not real now just because I'm freaking out." I spin around when something bumps into my back.

"It's just the lunch bag. It's okay. You're okay. Take a deep breath."

"Okay," I pant, then drag in a lungful of air, then another.

"Now, I need you to stay calm while I see if I can get the canoe empty so we can get it back to shore," he tells me, sounding way too damn calm.

"Right, sure. I can do that," I agree, and he lets me go. Not willing to be too far from him, I go with him, then help him turn the canoe back to upright in the water, which leaves the bottom half of the boat filled.

He looks around, then meets my gaze. "We gotta empty some of this or it's going to sink under our weight."

"How are we going to do . . . ?"

Before I can finish asking how he plans on making that happen, he grabs hold of the edge and starts to push and pull it with enough force that the water flies up and over the edge. I join in, pushing and pulling, and my arms start to ache.

"That should be enough." He stops and turns to me. "Put your foot in my hand, and then I want you to reach for the opposite edge of the boat and pull yourself in."

I look at his hands, then the edge of the boat that's now floating a few inches above my head. "How about I give you a boost?"

"Trust me."

"Fine," I mutter. Then I put my bare foot in his hand, the flip-flops I was wearing now floating somewhere or on the bottom of the lake. "Ready?" I ask as I grab hold of his shoulders.

"You've got this."

"I'm glad you think so," I grumble before I dive for the opposite edge of the canoe, catching it with the tips of my fingers. With sheer will, I somehow manage to get a good grip. Then, with Blake's help, I fall into the bottom of the boat. I turn to help him, but he's no longer where I left him. "Blake?" I yell and then spin around when he yells back to me.

"Just getting the paddles." He swims back toward me with both the wooden paddles in his hands. "We wouldn't get very far without these."

"Good thinking." I shiver, taking them from him and dropping them into the bottom of the boat.

"Watch out, baby. I'm coming in," he says right before he pops up over the side of the canoe like some kind of ninja, and I grab hold of each side of the boat, positive we're going to end up in the water again. "Do you still want to have lunch?" he asks me, using the end of one of the paddles to grab the soft-sided cooler and pull it up out of the water.

"No, I think I'll pass." I laugh, covering my face.

"Figures," he says with a chuckle, and I snort, which makes him laugh harder. "Mom's going to be disappointed."

"She will be," I agree, because one thing I've learned quickly is that Janet loves feeding people, especially the people she cares about.

"You're shivering. Let's get you back to the house and warmed up."

"That sounds like a great idea," I agree. "Just so you know, I think this is going to be my last canoe trip."

"Come on, it's been fun," he says as he starts to row us back toward the dock, and I study his smile and the lightness in his expression. It might not have been fun ending up in the water, but seeing him relaxed once more has made it worth it. "Dad's at the dock."

I look over my shoulder and see that Dave is in fact standing at the end of the dock, with Margret, Janet, and the kids all on the grass just onshore. "They probably saw us go in the water."

"If you two wanted to go swimming, you should have just jumped off the dock!" Dave shouts with a wide smile on his face.

"Your son was trying to use me as bait to get the Flathead Monster to show itself!" I yell back, and he laughs loud while I hear Margret and Janet both do the same.

"He's still after that speedboat, I see," he says, and Blake chuckles while I grin. When we reach the dock a minute later, Dave reaches down to help me out of the canoe, but I notice his hands are shaking, so I avoid his hand and use the edge of the dock to pull myself up, then kind of roll out onto the wooden planks.

"I'm never leaving dry land again," I pant, looking up at Dave, and he smiles before turning to offer Blake help getting out. Like me, Blake doesn't take Dave's hand, probably worried the two of them might end up in the water. And unlike me, he gets out of the boat with ease. As he ties it up to the dock, I get up and take off my life vest, then hear Janet gasp.

"You're bleeding."

"I'm okay, just a scratch," I assure her, then look at Sam when he calls for me. "Mommy went for a swim."

"Wim," he gurgles while he kicks his legs and claps. "Da, da, wim."

"Yeah, buddy, we both went for a swim," Blake tells him, wrapping his arm around my shoulders. "Now, we need to shower."

"How did you two end up in the water anyway?" Margret asks as we head up the stairs that lead to the house from the edge of the water.

"Blake was telling me about the monster in the lake; then something jumped out of the water, and I panicked, trying to get away before it carried me overboard."

"Oh Lord." She giggles. "Did you really think it was the monster?"

"I didn't know what it was." I laugh. "All I knew is it wasn't going to take me."

"It was probably just a fish," Janet chimes in. "And if it was the monster, all your screaming surely scared it off."

"Probably," I agree.

"I heard you yelling from all the way in the house." Dave chuckles. "I thought for sure that someone was being attacked."

"I *was* being attacked, or at least that's what I'm going to tell anyone who asks."

"You might want to fill me in on this story we're telling people. That way our accounts will match," Blake says, and I tip my head back to look up at him.

"We'll keep it simple." I shrug. "We were out canoeing when the Flathead Lake Monster toppled our boat. Thankfully, I thought quickly and got us both out of the water before it could drag us to its secret cave and feed us to its babies."

"That's your 'simple' story?" he asks, making air quotes while his lips tip up.

"That's the story I'm going with," I tell him as I enter the house behind Dave; then I turn to Janet, who still has ahold of Sam. "Do you mind watching him for a few minutes more while I shower?"

"Of course not. Go ahead. We'll be here when you get back."

"Thank you," I tell her, giving him a quick kiss on his cheek before making my way past the kitchen and down the hall to my bedroom, with Blake on my heels. "Do you want to go first?" I ask him before I head into my room to grab something dry to put on.

"You can go first."

"Thanks." I give him a smile, then quickly grab some clothes from my room and head across the hall, but when I start to shut the door to the bathroom, Blake stops me.

"Maybe we should try to conserve the hot water in case anyone else needs to shower."

"That would be the nice thing to do."

"That's what I was thinking." He grins, and I bite my lip and look down the hall before letting him into the small room. As he turns on the shower, I strip out of my wet clothes; then, while he gets undressed, I slip under the hot spray. A moment later, he joins me, and even though the shower is quick, we both get out completely satisfied.

∼

Like last night, with Sam now asleep and his monitor on the table near me, I sit out on the deck with my feet curled under me, watching the sky get darker by the minute. I smile to myself when I hear Margret laughing from inside the house, and I know if I were to turn around, I would see Blake, his parents, and his sister at the counter in the kitchen, playing Yahtzee together.

"Why are you hiding out here?" Dave asks, making me jump, and I turn to look at him over my shoulder, then watch him walk toward me.

"Not hiding, just giving you guys some family time," I tell him as he comes over and takes a seat on the chair across from where I'm sitting. When he groans and holds his hand over his stomach, I bite my lip. "I know you know," he says quietly after a moment, and I hold my breath. "I'm glad he told you. I hate that he's been keeping it to himself."

"You told him to," I remind him, trying to keep the bite out of my tone, and he nods.

"You're right; I did." He sighs.

"Why?"

"Denial, guilt, anger, depression, and a whole lot more denial." He leans his head back and closes his eyes. "I thought I'd beat it. I convinced myself that I would and that no one would have to know, and if they did find out, it wouldn't matter, because I would have been free and clear." He meets my gaze. "It did not go as planned."

"Blake knows you took him off your contact list for the doctor."

"Yeah, that was my last-ditch effort to protect him."

"But you're not protecting him. You're hurting him," I say, then wish I didn't, because his eyes open, and the pain I see shining back at me is almost unbearable to witness.

"I love my family."

"They love you," I tell him quietly, and he nods once. "I . . ." I clear my throat. "I know it isn't my place, but I would want to know. If you were my dad or my husband, I would want to know."

"Why? It's not going to change anything; it's just going to be a shadow hanging over every moment we have together."

Oh God, my throat gets so tight it burns as I swallow. "I'd still want to know. I'd want to know so I didn't have regrets, like missing dinner or a phone call or a picture. I wouldn't want to look back and think I missed out on something, when it had been right there at my fingertips."

"Maybe you're right," he says after a moment; then he looks toward the house and stands up. "I'm gonna call it a night."

"Sure," I whisper, tipping my head back to look up at him when his hand lands on my shoulder.

"I've never seen my son as happy or content as he's been since you and Sam came into his life." His fingers tighten. "I'm glad he found you, that he'll have you to help him get through things."

Without a clue of what to say, I nod, and he lets me go. I turn and watch him head into the house. Then, with tears making my vision blurry, I watch him kiss his wife before saying something that makes his son and daughter both laugh. Wiping away the tears on my cheeks, I know in that moment that I'm all in, that even with the risk of ending up with my heart broken, there is no going back.

Chapter 15

EVERLY

"You need to be nice," I hear Janet say in a tone I haven't heard from her before, and my brows drag together as I walk toward the kitchen with Sam on my hip.

"I'm not going to be a dick to the guy," Blake grumbles, sounding so much like his old cranky self that I stop in my tracks. How in the world had I forgotten how grumpy he could be? It's like I mentally blocked out the jerk he was and probably still is to other poor, unsuspecting strangers.

"Good, you're here." Janet's eyes come to where I'm standing. "I was just telling Blake that his grandma and her boyfriend are on their way."

"Awesome." I walk toward Blake, and he gives me a look that states clearly that he does not think it's awesome. "Do you want me to help get anything ready for them?" I ask Janet while Blake reaches for Sam, who is now chanting "Da, da, da" like he hasn't seen him for years, when he just saw him right before his nap.

"About that." She looks between Blake and me as I grab a banana for Sam. "I know you two have been sharing a room."

Oh my God. I feel my stomach bottom out, and I brace for the lecture I'm sure is coming, one I'm positive will involve her pointing out that I have a kid, so we shouldn't be sleeping together.

"I was wondering if it would be okay to put Grandma and Lance in the room next to you, so they don't have to stay in the entertainment room on the pullout."

"Sure," I agree quickly, feeling relieved while Blake glowers at his mom. "Stop." I elbow him, and he turns his head my way.

"Do you want to listen to my grandma and her boyfriend getting it on all night?"

"Oh my goodness, that's not going to happen!" Janet cries while I roll my eyes at him.

"What's not going to happen?" Margret asks while she walks across the kitchen to the fridge.

"Nothing," Janet says quickly. Then she asks, "What does everyone want for dinner? I was thinking we could get the stuff to make lasagna."

"That sounds good to me." Margret comes over with a can of Coke and leans into the counter next to her mom. "Do you mind if Mason comes? He's at his parents' in Ravalli."

"You've talked to Mason since we've been here?" Blake asks her, sounding like an overprotective big brother. I grab his thigh and squeeze in a silent reminder that he needs to tread carefully, because he might not remember the conversation we had about his sister's love life, but I do.

"I talk to him every day." She shrugs like it's not a big deal, and Janet pats her hand, then looks at Blake.

"Mason is family. He's always invited."

"Cool." Margret kisses her mom's cheek. "I'll let him know." She pushes away from the counter, then bounces out of the kitchen, saying over her shoulder, "I'm going to wake up Taylor so she's not up all night."

"All right, now can you go to the store to get the stuff for dinner?" she asks Blake, grabbing a pad of paper and a pen from the drawer.

"Sure." He looks at me. "Do you feel like going into town?"

"I'm not going to pass up a chance to go to that coffee shop in the grocery store." I shrug, taking Sam back from him so I can go get him dressed, since all he has on is a onesie proclaiming him *The Man*. "I'll be back in just a few minutes."

"All right." He kisses the side of my head before I slip off the stool. When I get back to the kitchen, Margret lets me know Janet has gone outside to read and Blake is out moving around vehicles, since his truck is blocked in.

I go out to meet him with Sam, and when we get outside, I find him on the phone, standing at the end of the driveway. When he sees me, he hangs up with whoever he's talking to and comes to take Sam from me, the look on his face hard to read.

"That was Tanner. He and Cybil want us to come for dinner. I told them I'd let them know when we can both make it."

"They know about us, that we're together?"

"Are they not supposed to?" He raises a brow.

"No, I just . . ."

"You just what?"

"I don't want things at work to be weird."

"Babe, you might have missed it, but Tanner and Mav have been pushing us at each other and waiting for this to happen, because they knew it was inevitable."

"Oh." I bite my lip. "In that case, it'll be fun. I can't wait to meet Claire," I say as he slides Sam's diaper bag off my shoulder, shaking his head like he thinks I'm cute. "Did he say anything else?"

"Just asked if I've talked to Mav."

"Has he?"

"Nope, not a word."

"And he still hasn't responded to your texts?"

"No." He shuts the back door of his truck after he gets Sam in his seat, then runs fingers through his hair. "The only thing I can think is he decided to go to his cabin and has no service."

"I think you should go check on him," I tell him honestly. "I mean, I totally get the need to decompress after a difficult trip, but it seems odd to me that he's not returning any phone calls or messages."

"Yeah." He helps me into my seat. "His cabin isn't very far from here. I'll head up there to check on him when we get back from the store."

I narrow my eyes on his as I tuck my feet into the cab. "Is that going to be your excuse to get out of spending time with your grandma and her boyfriend?" I ask, and he grins in answer, making me roll my eyes.

~

"I should have fucking pretended to get lost coming back from Mav's cabin," Blake whispers under his breath as he shifts on his chair.

"Too late," I whisper back, resting my hand on his thigh while watching Sandy, his grandma, and Lance, her boyfriend, who are seated across the table from us. The two of them are completely oblivious to how uncomfortable it is being around them as they whisper, kiss, and laugh like they're the only people in the room. Honestly, though, if they weren't making things so awkward, I would think they're cute together.

"I need a glass of wine," Margret announces suddenly, pushing back from the table, and I tip my head back to look at her when she rests her hand on my shoulder. "Do you want a glass?"

"Sure, thanks."

"No problem." She looks at Sandy. "Grandma?"

"Lance and I will go with you and see if your mama and daddy need any help with dinner." Sandy gets up, with Lance following her lead; then the three of them leave the room. I turn to Blake to see his frown firmly in place, his eyes on the door.

"They're gone. You can stop frowning for a minute and give your muscles a break," I tell him, and he meets my gaze.

"Does Margret seem off to you?"

"I think everyone is off, watching your grandma. I thought you were overexaggerating, but you were not."

"No, it's not that. She loves Lance and that Grandma found him."

"Oh." I glance to the door, realizing she hasn't been her happy-go-lucky self since we got back with groceries. "Now that you mention it, she did seem a little off when we got back from the store."

"That's what I was thinking. I wonder." He shakes his head, and I raise a brow.

"Wonder what?"

"I called Mason when I found that Mav wasn't at his cabin to see if he's heard from him. He told me he hadn't. He also mentioned he was going on a date when I asked if he was coming to dinner."

"Oh." I glance at the door. "Does Margret know that?"

"Yeah, he said he mentioned it to her," he says, and my heart sinks. "Do you think that's why she's upset?"

"Honestly?" I ask, and he nods. "Yes . . . if she knows that he has a date, she's probably more hurt than she thought she would be, and maybe even confused." I give his thigh a squeeze. "I mean, I know they're friends, but I also think there are deeper feelings there that maybe neither of them has been willing to act on because of Taylor's dad and Mason's loyalty to you."

"I should talk to her." He starts to stand, but I stop him before he can.

"No, you shouldn't."

"Why not?"

"Because she needs time to work out how she's feeling, and all that you talking to her is going to do is make her defensive."

"I'm not going to attack her."

"I know you're not, but I'm sure you've always made it clear you would be upset if she wanted to date one of your friends, so she will not accept that you're somehow okay with it now. Plus, she might not even realize that's what she wants."

"So what do I do?" he asks, sounding unsure, and my face softens.

"Nothing," I say quietly, touching my fingertips to the edge of his jaw. "I know that goes against everything that makes you *you*, but really, Margret needs to deal with this situation on her own."

"I don't like the idea of her hurting."

"I know, but give her a little time to work through her feelings before you jump in to save the day."

His eyes scan mine, and I can tell that he's torn, so I'm surprised when he says, "Okay."

"Mom is taking the lasagna out of the oven," Margret says a second later, and I look up at her as she places a glass of red wine on the table next to me.

"Does she need any help?" I ask.

"Nope, between Dad, Lance, and Grandma, I think she's covered." She takes a seat, then gulps down almost half her glass.

"I should go wake up Sam." I start to get up, but Blake stops me.

"I'll go get him."

"Are you sure?"

"Yeah." He touches his lips to my temple, then gets up and walks out of the room.

"He's in love with you," Margret says softly, and my heart flutters inside my chest as I turn to look at her, and I open my mouth to deny it. "And don't even bother saying he's not." She waves her hand and takes another gulp of wine. "I know him better than anyone, maybe even better than he knows himself, and without a doubt, he's in love with Sam and you."

"I . . ." God, what do I say to that? I can't say I love him too. Even if this feels a lot like love, I have to be realistic. We hardly know each other. "We haven't even been together long."

"What does time have to do with love?" She shakes her head. "I bet you fell in love with Sam before you even met him."

"That's different."

"No, that's love. Sometimes, it hits you in an instant, and other times, it builds slowly. However it happens, it's never in your control." She wraps an arm around her waist, leans back in her chair, and takes another sip of her wine. I want to ask her if that's what happened with Mason, if her feelings have built up over time without her even knowing it. It would make sense—she and Mason have always been friends, and sometimes it's difficult to see what's right in front of you.

"Who's ready to eat?" Janet asks as she comes into the room. She sets a large glass dish on the table, the smell of cheese and garlic making my mouth water. "Where did Blake go?" She looks at the empty chair next to me.

"He went to get Sam," I tell her, and she nods as Dave comes in, carrying Taylor in one hand and a basket of bread in the other. His mom follows with a big bowl of salad, and Lance has two glasses of wine.

"It looks and smells delicious, Mom." Blake walks into the room with a still-sleepy Sam, and my heart warms as he comes back to take his seat with Sam cuddled against his chest, completely content to stay in his arms.

"All right, dig in," Janet orders, and I make a plate for myself and one for Blake, and like we tend to do, we both take turns feeding Sam small bites.

"So, Lance and I have an announcement," Sandy says, picking up her glass, and Lance wraps his arm around her shoulders. "Lance and I are getting married."

"What?" Dave asks, sounding confused.

"We're getting married," she repeats, lifting her hand, and I notice the simple gold band on her finger. "We're thinking Vegas might be fun. Everyone could fly out for a weekend; then Lance and I will stay a few extra days as a little honeymoon." She looks around the table, which has grown completely quiet. "Isn't anyone going to say congratulations?"

"Congratulations," I tell them, feeling Blake's eyes on me, but I ignore him and pick up my glass to raise it before I take a sip.

"Yeah, congrats, Grandma," Margret says.

"Aren't you happy for us?" Sandy asks Dave, and he shakes his head.

"Of course we're all happy for you both," Janet cuts in before Dave can respond. "I think we're just all a little caught off guard."

"Your father passed away fifteen years ago, David," Sandy says, keeping her eyes locked on her son. "I deserve to have someone in my life that makes me happy. Your dad would have wanted me to be happy."

"It's not that, Mom." He sighs, and I take another sip from my glass, not sure if it's the situation or the wine that's making me feel hot.

"Then what is it? Is it because Lance is younger than I am?"

"No, it's not that, and I am happy for you," Dave tells her.

"You don't look very happy." She turns her eyes to Blake. "Neither do you."

"Grandma, I love you, and if marrying Lance is going to be what makes you happy, go for it. That doesn't mean I need to jump for joy that you're marrying a guy you hardly know."

"How well do you know Everly and that sweet baby boy in your arms?" she asks him, and I bite my lip. "As far as I know, you haven't known them very long, yet here Everly is, sitting at this table with your family, and there you are, holding her son like he's yours."

"She's got you there, brother," Margret says, grabbing the bottle of wine off the table before dumping what's left into her glass and mine.

"This life is short," Sandy says softly, glancing at everyone. "I spent years thinking I didn't have the right to find someone after losing my Ken. I thought I used up all the happiness meant for me; then Lance came along." She turns to look at her fiancé, her face softening, making her look years younger. "I'm happy again." She glances around the table once more as Blake's fingers lock with mine. "Really happy because of him, and I want you all to be happy for me too."

Dave clears his throat, and I watch him look at Janet, his expression filled with so much pain that I feel my nose start to sting. I can only imagine that he's thinking about what might happen if he leaves her behind and that she might one day feel like his mom did.

"You're right, Mom." His gaze goes to Sandy. "You do deserve to be happy, and I am happy for you." He looks at Lance. "I'm happy for both of you, and Vegas sounds like fun. You let us know when you want to go, and we'll work out arrangements with everyone."

"Thank you, honey." Sandy reaches for his hand and covers it with her own; then she looks at Blake, and I brace, not sure what he will say or do.

"You both have my support," he tells them, and I pick up my glass of wine to hide the fact that tears have filled my eyes.

Thankfully, the rest of dinner is filled with light conversation and lots of laughs as Janet, Dave, and Sandy tell stories about Margret and Blake when they were growing up. When we're all done eating, Margret and I clean up the kitchen while Blake and Dave keep an eye on the kids; then we all head out to the back deck, where we sit around the fire, roasting marshmallows and talking until it's time to go to bed.

After brushing my teeth, I head across the hall to the bedroom that Blake and I have been sharing, then stop at the side of Sam's crib and place his blanket back over him.

"He keeps kicking it off," Blake tells me, and I turn to smile at him. He's sitting up in bed without a shirt on, a view I've gotten used to over the last couple of days. "Come here, Everly." He holds out his hand, and I go to him and take his hand, allowing him to pull me down to straddle him. "I gotta tell you I'm not looking forward to going home tomorrow."

"Me neither." I smooth my finger between his brows. "This trip was way too short."

"It was." His hands find their way under the sleep tank I have on. "It's gonna suck not waking up to you and Sam every morning."

"Yeah, but just think: you'll be able to sleep through the entire night without waking up," I remind him, because every night when Sam has woken up, he's gotten up with me, even though I've told him he doesn't have to.

"No, now I'm going to be thinking about the fact that you're going to be getting up, and I won't be there."

I tip my head to the side. "It really doesn't bother you, does it?"

"What?"

"Me having a kid?"

"No, why would it?"

"I don't know." I bite the inside of my cheek. "I guess I just worry that one day you might realize that having a girlfriend with a kid is way too much responsibility. I mean, it's not like we'll ever really get alone time, and it will never be easy for me to just get up and go on a date with you, or for us to have a weekend away."

"I love having Sam around. I don't find it a hardship to spend time with him, and if I was ever worried about any of that, I wouldn't have started something with you. I knew what I was getting into, and I'm not walking into this blind. I want this: you, Sam, and I," he says firmly, leaving no room for me to question if he's being truthful.

I rest my forehead against his. "I have no idea how I'm going to sleep without you after tonight," I admit, and his face softens.

"Me neither, baby, which means you're going to have to get comfortable with the idea of you and Sam staying with me when you can . . . or every night," he says, and I laugh.

"I'm sure we can work something out." I smile as he rolls me to my back; then he kisses the smile off my face and tucks me into his side before reaching over to shut off the light.

"Night, baby."

"Night." I curl deeper into him; then, as I listen to his breathing even out, I drift off to sleep, happy, content, and safe in his arms.

Chapter 16

EVERLY

When I pull up to the lodge, I put my car in park and shut off the engine, then grab my bag off the passenger seat and get out. I send Blake a message letting him know I'm heading into the office. He sends me a message back, telling me he's going to be here in about an hour and that when he gets in, we'll call Ginny and Jeff's lawyer to set up a time to meet with them.

Yesterday on the way home from the lake house, he and I talked at length about the pros and cons of meeting with Ginny and Jeff again, and by the time we got to my parents' place, we agreed I should give them one more chance. Or, I should say, I convinced him that I should give them another chance, because he made it clear he does not want Sam or me anywhere near them. The only thing that made him feel a little better about it was when I agreed that he could be with me at the meeting and that Sam would stay with my mom.

I text him back, reminding him he doesn't need to be around when I call, and he messages back in all caps WAIT FOR ME, which is exactly what he said earlier this morning when we were on a video call.

With a sigh, I let myself into the building and head to the kitchen to make a pot of coffee, needing some extra caffeine. Last night, as I predicted would happen, Sam didn't sleep very well. Then again, neither did I. It's crazy how quickly I've gotten used to falling asleep curled into Blake, especially when I was never a cuddler before him.

After I have my cup of coffee, I walk through the lodge to the office and stop in my tracks when I see Maverick sitting at my desk, looking alive and perfectly well.

"Hey," he says simply, sparing me a quick glance before shutting down the web page he was looking at.

"Hey," I repeat, then shake my head. "What are you doing here? Where have you been?"

"I've been out of town." He stands up and moves around the desk as I set down my bag. "And I work here." He grins.

"Don't be funny. Everyone has been worried about you. Have you talked to Blake?" I plop down in my chair while he takes a seat across from me.

"I just sent him a message. I lost my cell and haven't had a chance to replace it." He leans back in his chair. "I saw his text about you two heading to the lake house with his family. How was that?"

"Good, it was nice to get away, and it's beautiful there."

"It is," he agrees. "Did you have a chance to go out on the lake?"

"Unfortunately," I say, and he laughs.

"That bad?"

"Blake and I ended up in the water after he told me the story of the lake monster, and a fish jumped out of the water, scaring me half to death."

"I wish I had been there to see that."

"I'm sure you'll hear all about it in detail." I smile when he laughs, then tip my head to the side. "Are you sure you're okay? We've been worried."

"I'm good." He raises his arms above his head to stretch. "I just needed a break." He pushes up to stand. "Is there more coffee in the kitchen?"

"Yep, a fresh pot."

"Cool, gonna grab a cup, check out some stuff, then run to town to get a new phone."

"Okay, I'll be here if you need anything," I tell him, and he jerks up his chin before disappearing. I grab my cell and send Blake a message, letting him know Maverick is back, then put my phone aside and get to work.

With a cup of coffee in hand, I read over the email I just typed up to make sure everything is spelled correctly and that all the questions that were asked were addressed. Once I'm sure it's good, I press send and sit back, taking a sip from my mug. Even with all the work I have to catch up on, being away for a few days was still worth it.

"All right, let's do this," Blake says, stepping into the office, and I set down my cup and let out a breath as he comes around the desk.

"I told you that you didn't need to be here when I call. I know you've got stuff to do," I tell him as he touches his fingers to my chin, tipping my head back so he can plant a kiss on my lips.

"And I told you that I want to be." He lets me go and takes a seat on the edge of my desk, then pushes my cell phone toward me. "So let's do this and get it over with."

"Fine." I pick it up, then dial the number I saved for Lucas and put my phone on speaker. As it rings, my leg bounces up and down, and my fingers tap the top of the desk.

"It's going to be okay."

"I know."

I tip my head back to look at him when a very chirpy woman answers: "Greenburn Family Law, Lillian speaking. How may I help you?"

"Hi, Lillian, this is Everly Standler. I'm calling to speak with Lucas."

"Hi, Everly, please hold, and I'll connect you," she says; then the line goes quiet for a moment.

"Everly, it's nice to hear from you," Lucas says as he comes on the line. "I'm guessing you had time to think about coming in to meet with Ginny and Jeff."

"I did, and . . ." I let out a breath. "And after thinking about it, I'm willing to meet with them one more time, but I'd like the counselor to be in the room with us along with my boyfriend."

"I think that's an acceptable request," he says. "Do you have a day or a time that would work best for you both to come into the office?"

"Do you know how long this will take?"

"It shouldn't be more than an hour."

"Okay, I'm going to put you on hold for a minute to look at the calendar."

"Sure," he says, and I place the call on mute, then look up at Blake.

"When can you go with me?" I ask, knowing that it's going to be more difficult for him to get away than it is for me.

"Tomorrow morning is clear until ten. See if he can set it up before then; if not, we might have to schedule it for next week, after the next group leaves," he says, and I unmute the call.

"Hey, Lucas, tomorrow before ten works for us. If that's not okay with Ginny and Jeff, we will have to schedule a time for next week."

"Perfect, if you can hold for a second, I'll give Ginny a call and see if . . . let's say, eight thirty works for her."

"Sounds good," I reply, and the line goes quiet. I stare at the screen of my phone, questioning if I'm doing the right thing.

"I was thinking," Blake says, sliding his finger down my temple, then back behind my ear, grabbing my attention, and I focus on his handsome face. "When we leave here, I'll follow you to your parents', and we can take Sam to the park, then have dinner in town."

"I'd like that, and Sam will be happy about seeing you in person. He was cranky after his video call with you this morning."

"I missed him too." He opens his mouth like he's going to say more, but Lucas comes back on the line, cutting him off.

165

"Ginny says eight thirty works for her and Jeff, so I'll text you the address for the office when we hang up, and see you tomorrow morning."

"Great, see you then." I hang up after he says goodbye, then meet Blake's gaze. "Well, there's no going back now."

"We don't have to show up for the appointment," he points out; then his expression softens. "But I know you need to do this, and tomorrow, when it's over, you'll either have the closure you need or more people in your life who love Sam."

"You're right." I let out a breath, and he grabs my hand and pulls me up to stand in front of him. I fit myself between his spread thighs and rest my hands on his chest. "Did you see Maverick when you got here?"

"No, and his truck wasn't in the lot when I arrived. How did he seem when you talked to him?"

"Like himself. Do you think he was telling the truth about his phone?"

"Yeah, he's not one to lie about shit like that." His hands smooth up my arms, then curve around my neck so he can pull me closer. "Sucks that I gotta get back to work."

"Does it?" I drop my eyes to his mouth as I lean into him, and he grins, pulling me closer to touch his mouth to mine. The kiss starts out soft and sweet but heats up when his fingers slide into my hair, and I nip his lip. My lips part when his tongue touches my bottom lip, and before I know it, we're making out hot and heavy, with our hands roaming all over each other.

When his mouth trails down my neck, I cup him over his jeans, listening to him groan, then jerk back when Tanner walks into the office.

"Oh shit. Sorry," Tanner says, turning and heading right back out the door.

"It's okay!" I yell after him as I straighten my top and pat down my hair. "You don't have to leave."

"Are you sure?" He chuckles while Blake adjusts himself and moves to stand behind my chair, probably in an attempt to hide his erection.

"Yep." I grab my coffee and down a gulp of it as he walks back into the room.

"If the door had been shut, I would have knocked." He grins, taking a seat, then looks at Blake over my shoulder. "You want some ice, man?"

"Funny," Blake grumbles. Then he asks, "What are you doing here?"

"I got a message from Mav this morning saying he lost his phone but that he was here. I had to go to the grocery store, so I figured I'd stop by to check on him."

"I think he's out getting a new cell phone now," I tell him. "Are Cybil and the baby home, or did you bring them with you?"

"They're home." The look on his face changes, and it's so beautiful, because I know it's because he's thinking of his wife and daughter. "Cybil's still in some pain after the C-section, and Claire's still sleeping most of the time, so they're just hanging in bed."

"Well, let me know if you need help with anything, even if you want me to come over so you guys can take a nap." I smile. "I remember how little sleep you get during those first few weeks."

"Thanks, I appreciate that. Cybil's best friend and her mom are here now, and with the two of them around, Cybil and I have to fight for time with Claire."

I laugh. "A blessing and a curse."

"Yeah." He smiles and looks at Blake as he comes around the desk to sit down; then his eyes come back to me. "So I'm guessing things with you two are good."

"Don't start," Blake rumbles while my cheeks warm.

"So don't give you shit about your relationship with Everly the way you gave me shit about me and Cybil getting together?"

"I would appreciate, if you do give him shit, that you do it when I'm not around," I say, and he looks at me and laughs. "I'm serious."

"I know." He gets up, then pats Blake on the shoulder. "I'm gonna head into town so I can get back home to my girls."

"I'll walk you out." Blake stands, then comes around to me, and I tip my head back when he leans down to give me a kiss. "Call and let me know when you're about ready to head home, and I'll make sure I'm back to follow you to your parents'."

"Okay, I'll let you know." I accept one more kiss, then look at Tanner. "Give Cybil and Claire hugs from me."

"Will do." He gives me a salute, then heads out the door with Blake on his heels. With the two of them gone, I pick up my phone and call my mom to let her know that Blake and I will be meeting Ginny and Jeff tomorrow morning; then I tell her our plans for dinner. Before I hang up, I somehow end up agreeing to her and Dad joining us, which should make tonight a little more interesting than it would have been otherwise.

∼

"Baby, you can't eat all of that." I laugh when Sam grabs a hunk of bread out of my hand and attempts to shove the whole thing into his mouth.

"No, no, no, da, da," he cries, throwing himself back against Blake's chest as I wrestle it from his grasp.

"Sorry, baby, but you can only have a little bite." I break off a small piece and place it into his mouth. He garbles something as he chews it up and reaches for more, then gets annoyed when I only give him another small bite.

"I don't blame him—I want to shove all the bread into my mouth too," Mom says, dipping a chunk into the olive oil and balsamic mixture that's in a little dish on the table, and Dad chuckles next to her.

"The only reason I'm not eating it all is because I know I'll regret filling up on bread when my dinner gets here," I tell her as Blake saves his beer from being knocked over by Sam's fist when he reaches for the bread basket. "Maybe we should put him in the chair," I suggest.

"I got him," he says, and I shake my head at him.

"I know you got him, but I think it will be easier if he's in the chair," I tell him, and he wraps his hand around the back of my neck, massaging it while also ignoring me. I roll my eyes, then meet my mom's gaze and see the smile on her face.

"So are you prepared for the meeting tomorrow morning?" Dad asks, picking up his glass of whiskey, and I shrug.

"I don't know if I'm prepared, but I want it done and over with. I just hope that Ginny doesn't say anything about Sam not being Lex's again, because I might just lose my mind if she does."

"I know you said you don't want me to go with you, but I don't mind showing up."

"I know." I give Sam another piece of bread. "I just . . . I know you have to work and—"

"Everly May Standler," he says, cutting me off. "Your mom and I have made it clear that we are here for you. You're not a burden; you're our child." He looks at Sam. "Think about how you would feel if Sam were in this situation. You'd want to be there for him, and you'd never consider it a hindrance to have his back."

I look at Sampson, who I know I will always do everything in my power to protect, no matter his age. "You're right," I say softly, meeting my dad's gaze.

"I know I am." Dad shakes his head.

"Okay then, I would like you to be there." His shoulders visibly relax, and Mom pats his chest while giving me a look that clearly says she's as relieved as my dad is. "I'm sorry for not asking you to come sooner."

"You asked now, so it's done," Dad says simply, which I know means he's not open to me saying more about it.

169

"Dinner is served." Our waitress breaks into the moment, stopping at the edge of the table with a large tray covered with steaming dishes, and a man behind her places a stand for her to rest it on. After she passes things around the table, we settle into a conversation about the lodge and work and everyday life.

By the time dinner is done and we get Sam into his seat in Blake's truck, he's half-asleep, so Blake drives us back to my parents', then helps me get him upstairs and tucked into bed. I walk him back out, and he reminds me that he'll be here early in the morning to pick me up. He kisses me goodbye and takes off.

~

"Your dad is already here?" Blake asks me as he pulls into the parking lot in front of the Greenburn Family Law office. I look up from my cell phone to find my dad standing next to his car, wearing a suit and tie with his hair slicked back—a drastic change from his normal jeans and plaid shirts he wears to the office daily.

"He really went all out." I wave at my dad as we park next to him.

"Maybe I should have dressed up," Blake says, and I turn toward him.

"Do you even have a suit?" I ask, trying to imagine him dressed up. I'm sure he'd look beyond handsome in a suit. Then again, he looks handsome all the time.

"I do, I just doubt it fits me now." He chuckles, making me laugh, and I unhook my seat belt as my dad opens my door.

"Ginny and Jeff are already inside." He takes my hand and helps me down from the truck. "Are you ready?"

"As ready as I'm going to be." I reach for Blake's hand when he comes around the back of the truck to meet me; then I hold on to him with all my might as we walk to the building. My stomach churns when we get inside, and if it weren't for the hold that Blake has on my hand, I don't know that I wouldn't turn around and run right back out the door.

"Everly." A young, good-looking guy with blond hair and my dad's normal outfit of jeans and a button-down shirt appears from a hallway and walks toward me with his hand out. "I'm Lucas." He shakes my hand, then turns to Blake, who introduces himself. Lucas then moves to my dad and shakes his hand. "Ginny and Jeff are already here. We're just waiting on the counselor to arrive. As soon as she gets in, we'll head on back to the conference room." He looks among us. "In the meantime, feel free to help yourselves to a cup of coffee or a bottle of water."

"Thank you."

"No problem." He walks back down the hall, and I watch my dad make some coffee while I take a seat with Blake on the couch.

"Relax," Blake whispers and then grabs my thigh, which is bouncing like crazy, and I cover his hand with mine. "It's going to be okay."

"I know. It's just . . . I'm having flashbacks to the last time that we met with them."

The front door then opens, and an older woman wearing a flowy skirt with a sweater and about a dozen scarves around her neck walks inside.

"Hi." She waves as she passes us to head down the hall; then, a moment later, Lucas comes out.

"We're ready, if you guys are."

A sense of dread fills the pit of my stomach as I stand, and each step I take toward the conference room is like moving through concrete. When we get into the room, Jeff and Ginny are sitting on one side of the table, with the counselor seated at the head of it. I take a seat between my dad and Blake and look anywhere but at Lex's parents.

"Good morning, everyone. My name is Ava." The counselor smiles brightly. "I think we should all go around the table and introduce ourselves," she says, so we all introduce ourselves, and when we're done, she looks at all of us. "Lucas explained a little of this situation to me, but I'd like to hear from you guys what you think the best-case scenario would be when it comes to visitation, then the worst." She meets my gaze. "Everly, would you go first?"

"Sure." I clear my throat. "I think the best case would be Sam having a relationship with his biological grandparents and being able to lean on them if he has questions about his father's side of his family as he gets older." I bite my lip, then continue. "The worst would be him not having that option, then feeling like he was missing out as he grows up."

"So him having a connection is important to you."

"A healthy connection, yes," I clarify, and she nods.

"Now, Ginny, would you like to go?"

"Yes," Ginny says, meeting my eye. "But first, I would like to apologize," she says, and Jeff wraps his arm around her shoulders. "When we met, I didn't know the full story of what happened between you and my son, and I made some really hurtful assumptions. I'm sorry for that." I nod, letting her know I heard her, and I swear it looks like tears fill her eyes. "The best-case scenario would be for us to have a chance to spend time with our only grandson." She clears her throat, then grabs a tissue from a box on the table in front of her. "The worst would be not knowing him but knowing he exists."

"So it sounds like you're all on the same page," Ava says softly, and I nod, because it does sound like that is the case.

"Now let's talk about what a visitation arrangement would look like. What would make you feel most comfortable, Everly?"

"I don't know. I guess . . . I would want to be there," I say, and Ava nods.

"And how do you feel about that?" She looks at Ginny and Jeff.

"We would be completely okay with that," Jeff answers for both of them, then looks at me. "We are willing to do whatever you need us to."

"Okay," I say quietly, looking between him and Ginny.

Thirty minutes later, when the meeting comes to an end, I walk out of the conference room holding Blake's hand, feeling lighter than I have in weeks. I don't know what the future will hold, but I do know I have done my part in making it possible for Sampson to know his grandparents. The rest is up to them. But no matter what, my son will grow up surrounded by people who love him and choose him every single day.

Chapter 17

EVERLY

Sitting on the floor with Sam playing blocks, I get up when I hear my phone ring in the kitchen. I grab it off the table where I left it and smile when I see Blake is calling.

"Please tell me you're back," I answer, listening to him laugh.

"I'm on my way to the lodge now. Just going to shower, then I'll be on my way to pick up you and Sam," he says as I walk back into the living room. "Are you packed?"

"Yep, all packed."

"Good, because I fucking miss you guys."

"We miss you," I tell him, not sure I'll be able to get used to him being away for days at a time when it's his turn to take out a group, which is where he's been for the last five days. The only thing that's gotten me through these last several days is the knowledge that Sam and I will be staying with him at his house for a few days.

"All right, baby, I'll see you in less than an hour."

"See you soon. Love you." I hang up, then stare at my phone, trying to figure out if I really just told him that I love him or if I imagined saying it.

"You okay, honey?" my mom asks, coming into the kitchen, and I lick my lips.

"I think I just told Blake that I love him."

"What?" She laughs, looking at me over her shoulder as she opens the fridge.

"I think I said *love you* to Blake," I tell her, and she shuts the door after grabbing the bottle of orange juice, then walks to the cupboard and takes down a glass.

"So?"

"So?" I repeat, blinking at her. "Mom, I told him I love him."

"Well, you do love him, so what's the problem?" she asks, looking at me like I'm crazy.

Maybe I am crazy.

"He should say it first. He should be the one to tell me first, right?"

"Is that some new rule the kids made up?"

"It should be if it isn't."

"Honey, why are you overthinking this?"

"Because until I said it, I didn't even know I loved him, and it's a huge fricking deal, and now I don't know how he feels. For all I know, he heard me say it and is now packing up my desk and going online to place an ad for a new office manager for the lodge."

"Wow, you're *really* overthinking this."

"Mom!" I cry, and she starts to laugh.

"Honey, he loves you. Just because he hasn't said it doesn't make it any less true."

"How do you know?"

"Because he's proven how he feels about you and Sam over and over again." She fills up her glass. "Take a breath, and don't overthink this. Tonight, after you get Sam to bed, you two can talk about it."

"Are you insane? There is no way I'm going to bring this up."

"Okay, don't bring it up." She shrugs, then looks to the front of the house when the doorbell goes off. "I'll get that. It might be the grocery order I put in." She heads to the front of the house. I hear the front door open, then hear her yell, "Everly!"

"Yeah?" I walk toward the front door, and my heart starts to pound when I see Blake standing in the entryway, looking as handsome as always, even though it's obvious he hasn't showered or shaved in days.

"I'll look after Sam," Mom says, sounding smug as she walks past me, but I can't take my eyes off Blake's.

I start to open my mouth to say something, but my brain seems to malfunction as he prowls toward me. I take a step back, then another. Before I can get any farther, his big body collides with mine and his fingers thread through my hair as his other hand wraps around my hip, then slides to the small of my back, pulling me flush against him. When his mouth crashes down on mine, I gasp, then melt into him as he deepens the kiss. Lost in him, I kiss him back, then whimper in disappointment when he drags his mouth from mine.

"I love you too." He presses his forehead against mine, and I close my eyes. "You and Sam, I love both of you so fucking much." Oh God, I'm going to cry. I latch onto him with both hands.

"We love you, too," I say, whispering the truth as I look into his beautiful eyes; then I lift my hand to touch his cheek, which is now covered with a thick layer of stubble. "You didn't shower."

"No, I knew you were probably freaking yourself out, so I wanted to come reassure you that you're not alone in how you feel," he says, and tears fill my eyes.

"I was only freaking out a little."

"Right." He smiles as he smooths his thumb across my cheek. "And now?"

"I'm good now," I tell him quietly, and he leans forward to touch his mouth to mine in a soft kiss, then pulls back when Sam starts yelling "Da, da, da!"

"Hey, big guy." He scoops up Sam when he runs to us, and then he smothers his cheeks with kisses, making him giggle. I watch the two of them, my heart overflowing, then look at where my mom is leaning against the wall with her arms crossed over her chest and a soft look in her eyes. A look that states clearly how happy she is that Sam and I both have a man like Blake, a good man, a man of honor and integrity, the kind of man any mother would want her daughter to find after she's gotten her heart broken.

~

Lying on the floor in Blake's living room between the couch and coffee table, with a trail of cushions, pillows, blankets, and big heavy books going from the kitchen, around the back of the couch, to the front of the fireplace, I laugh as I watch Edmond and Sam try to avoid getting eaten by Blake and me, as we are both lava monsters. Yesterday afternoon, when we got to Blake's house, Sam and I hung out while he showered; then the three of us went to his parents' for dinner before coming home and putting Sam to sleep, then spending some much-needed time alone. It was a good day, and today has been even better, waking up in my guy's arms, then having breakfast together with Sam, and now hanging with Edmond while Tina is in town running some errands.

"Don't touch the lava." I reach out for Sam's chubby thigh, and he giggles as Edmond helps him climb up onto the couch, and Tutu follows both boys, making them giggle louder.

"Don't come this way." Blake reaches over the back, trying to grab them, and Edmond and Sam screech in laughter, going over the arm of the couch, and I roll to my belly and crawl on the floor, following both of them as they make their way across the trail of cushions, laughing so hard they keep stumbling. When both of them try to zoom past me, I latch onto Edmond's ankle, and he falls to his bottom, while Sam attempts to help him by crawling on his chest, and Tutu bounces around. Laughing so hard my stomach hurts, I roll to my back, and Sam stumbles over to me before laying his head on my chest. I pat his bottom, then look up at Blake as he looms over us.

"I think we wore him out." I smile, and his face softens as he takes Sam from me so I can get up. Then he hands him back to me. "I think I should feed him some lunch, then put him down for a nap."

"Lunch is a great idea. I'm starving," Edmond says as he helps clean up the pillows and blankets off the floor, and both Blake and I laugh.

"I don't want you to starve to death, so when we're done with this, you can help get the pizza ready to put in the oven."

"Awesome."

I catch Edmond's grin as I head to the kitchen with Sam. "Do you want me to preheat the oven?" I ask, grabbing one of Sam's baby ravioli dishes he loves from the freezer, since he can't really eat pizza yet.

"Yeah, thanks, babe," he says, and I pop Sam's food in the microwave, then start it up. "I need to get him a high chair." He kisses the side of my head as he walks into the kitchen with Edmond, and I settle at the counter with Sam on my lap.

"I have one that can hook to the table. I'll bring it next time. I just didn't think about it."

"Or I can just get him a high chair," he repeats as he pulls out a premade pizza crust from the freezer. I don't argue; I like that he wants Sam to have a high chair here, that he wants us to be here so much that he will need one.

"Have you heard from Ginny this morning?" he asks while he pulls out toppings for the pizza. He places them on the counter, where Edmond is now putting sauce on the crust while I feed Sam.

"I haven't even checked my phone since this morning." I give Sam a bite of one of his raviolis, then laugh when he dances on my lap as he chews. "I hope they're okay with my idea of them coming to my parents' house for their first visit with Sam."

"Right now, they need to do what makes you feel comfortable. If they're not okay with it, they need to pretend to be okay with it."

"You're right." I try to give Sam another bite, but he shakes his head and reaches for his juice cup, which he shoves away after one sip.

"Baba, dada, baba." He waves his hand at Blake.

"I think he's ready to sleep." I get up and carry him around the island so I can toss his almost-empty dish in the trash.

"I'll make his milk."

"Thank you." I go to where Edmond is and peek over his shoulder at the pizza, which has enough cheese for ten people and tons of pepperoni. "That looks delicious, dude."

"Thanks." He grins at me, then looks at Blake when he comes over with a bottle. "I think it's ready to go in the oven."

"I think so too." Blake picks it up and carries it across to the oven.

"Promise you two won't eat all of that while I'm putting Sam to sleep," I tell Edmond, watching the cute smile that forms on his face.

"It's not good to make promises you can't keep, babe," Blake tells me while kissing Sam's cheek, making him laugh.

"You two are not going to eat a whole pizza."

"We're growing boys," Edmond says, and Blake chuckles.

"I just want one piece. That's half a piece from each of you."

"What do you think? Can we do that?" Blake asks him.

"I guess." Edmond sighs.

"Thanks." I laugh, kissing Blake before I leave them in the kitchen and head down the hall to the guest bedroom, where Sam's crib is set up.

A little over twenty minutes later as he's falling asleep, I hear what sounds like someone pulling up the driveway; then Tutu starts to bark outside. I hush Sam back to sleep, then place him in his crib. I wait until I know he's not going to wake back up before I grab his monitor and leave the room.

As I walk to the kitchen, the smell of burning pizza hits my nose, and I frown when I don't see Blake or Edmond but do see smoke beginning to fill the room. Thinking quickly, I turn off the oven, then grab two mitts and open the oven. Smoke billows out as I pull out the pizza and set it on the counter, noticing then that the cheese has melted off and burnt around the edge of the pan. Then I look at the ceiling when the smoke alarm starts to blare. Panicked that Sam is going to wake up, I search for a broom until I find one, then start to wave it in the air over my head in an attempt to get the smoke away from the alarm so it will shut off.

"What happened?" Blake shouts over the noise as he runs into the room, followed by his mom and sister, who both look like they were crying.

"You forgot the pizza," I tell him, passing the broom over, then helping his mom and sister open the windows to let out some of the smoke. When the alarm shuts off, I jog down the hall to check on Sam and find him still asleep, having moved to lie on his back. I cover him up once more, then shut the door and walk toward the kitchen, a sense of foreboding filling the pit of my stomach. The only reason I can think that Janet and Margret would come over and both look like they've been crying is because they know about Dave, and if they know about Dave, then there's a chance they know Blake didn't tell them about his diagnosis.

"Is Sam still sleeping?" Blake asks, meeting my gaze when I walk around the corner. I nod, then look at his mom and sister, who are both sitting at the counter. I glance around for Edmond. "He's out riding his bike," he says, reading my mind. "I told him he had fifteen minutes, which might give me enough time to put a new pizza in for him."

"Are you really talking about pizza right now?" Margret asks on a hiss, and I get closer to Blake, then reach for his hand. "Dad has cancer, and you're talking about fucking pizza."

"Margret," Janet whispers.

"What, Mom? This is fucked up. Not only has Dad been lying to us, but Blake has known all along and been living like everything is hunky-dory. Do you not see how messed up that is?"

"He hasn't been living like everything is hunky-dory," I say, stepping slightly in front of him. "This situation has been eating him up."

"Right." Margret stands. "I forgot that he's been so stressed about our dad that he hasn't been going to work or dating you or living life like it's all okay."

"That's not fair," I whisper.

"Babe, it's okay," Blake says, grabbing my hip.

"It's not okay," I tell him while holding Margret's gaze. "Your brother has been doing all he can to be there for not just your dad but you, your mom, his friends, and now me. He deserves to have things in life that make him happy just like you do, and I get that you're upset, you have a reason to be, but don't put that all on him." She looks away as Blake's fingers dig into my hip, making me wonder if I said too much.

"Why didn't you tell us?" Janet asks on a hitched breath, wiping the tears from her cheeks.

"I wanted to." Blake's fingers flex, then his hand slides up my waist. "I wanted to tell you every fucking day, but I didn't know how."

"You could have done it by opening your mouth and saying the words," Margret says, crossing her arms over her chest as I hear the back door open. Figuring that Edmond is back, I wonder what I should do, because he doesn't need to be a witness to this situation, especially when emotions are so high.

"Dad," Margret breathes, and I turn to see Dave coming around the corner, his face a mask of devastation.

"I figured you two would be here."

His focus is on Janet; then he looks at his daughter when she whispers, "Why? Why didn't you tell us before now, Dad?"

"Because I didn't want this." He lifts his arms away from his body. "I didn't want you or your mom crying or upset. I didn't want to hurt you like you're hurting now." He locks his gaze on Janet. "When my mom lost my dad to cancer, I saw how much it ate her up. I saw how much she suffered after losing him. I didn't want you to go through that. I never want that for you."

"You're my husband. You should have told me."

"I'm your husband, and it's my job to protect you." His voice is rough as he looks between his wife and daughter. "I thought I would be able to protect you from this. I was sure you would never have to know."

"You told Blake." Margret wipes at the tears on her cheeks.

"I did." He turns to look at his son. "And I'm sorry about that, so fucking sorry for putting that on you, for putting you in a situation where you had to lie to your mom and your sister. I'm sorry I wasn't able to protect you. I just . . . I needed you and knew you could handle everything without cracking."

"Dad." Blake's voice sounds as rough as his father's, and I cover his hand with mine.

"I never wanted to hurt anyone." Dave looks around the room. "I didn't want this; I didn't want you all upset and worried because of me."

"Of course we're going to worry. We love you," Janet tells him, getting up and walking toward her husband. "I've worried every time you've had a migraine or been sick, and every time you've had a hard time getting out of bed. I've worried every day, because every day, I've felt helpless to help you and because I knew you weren't telling me the truth."

"I'm sorry." He wraps his arms around her.

"I'm so mad at you." She sags against his chest, and Margret sobs, watching her parents embrace. With tears filling my eyes, I give Blake's hand a squeeze, and he lets me go and walks over to his sister, taking her into his arms.

My hands ball into fists as I watch the four of them, and I say a silent prayer that them having each other will make this situation a little more bearable and that they will find enough strength in each other to get through this time. They need each other now more than ever.

I quickly swipe the tears from my cheeks when I hear the back door open again. I go to catch Edmond before he can reach the kitchen, wanting Blake and his family to have some time alone. "Will you help me check on Sam?" I ask when I meet him in the hall, and he nods.

"Is everything okay?" he asks me softly, looking over his shoulder to the kitchen as he follows me.

"Yeah, honey, Blake and his family are just talking," I tell him as I usher him into the guest room, where I'm surprised to see Sam awake and sitting up quietly in the middle of the crib.

"How about we go outside for a few minutes," I suggest, picking up Sam when he stands up and reaches for me. "You can show us some cool tricks on your bike."

"Sure," he agrees, so I grab a pair of shoes and hoodie for Sam, then take both boys outside, where Sam and I watch him ride his bike in the driveway and cheer him on as Sam collects rocks and the dandelions growing in the grass.

I don't know how much time passes before Blake, his parents, and his sister emerge from the house, but with one look at the four of them, I can see they're going to make it through whatever happens next together.

"I'm sorry for yelling at you," Margret says as she walks to where I'm standing, and I hug her back as her arms close around me.

"It's okay," I tell her quietly, meeting Blake's gaze over her shoulder, and he holds my eye for a moment before looking down at his mom, who touches his shoulder.

"It's not." I hear the tears in Margret's voice as she squeezes me tighter. "Thank you for being here for my brother and for making my dad realize it was time to tell us." Her words stun me as she lets me go. "I'm going to head home."

"Are you going to be okay?" I ask quietly. "Do you want me to drive you?"

"I'll be okay—just take care of my brother." She gives me a sad smile, then hugs her brother and parents before heading to her car.

"Sorry for ruining your day," Janet says while picking up Sam, who babbles something and gives her a handful of grass.

"You didn't, and you never could," I tell her, and she reaches for my hand, giving it a warm squeeze.

"I'm glad my baby boy has you."

"I'm glad I have him, that I have all of you." I squeeze her hand back, then laugh when Sam grabs her face, shouting "Meme," the name he started calling her when we were at the lake house.

"Sorry, I know you want Grandma's attention, but I was talking to your mama." She laughs, hugging and kissing his cheeks and neck, making him giggle; then her gaze locks on mine, and tears fill her eyes.

"Please don't cry," I whisper.

"They're happy tears." She passes Sam back to me. "Take care of my babies."

"Will do," I promise as we walk to where Blake and Dave are talking quietly. As soon as we're close, both men turn their gaze our way, and I can tell with one look that the two are both relieved and terrified, which is understandable, given what happened.

"Are you ready to go home?" Dave asks as Janet curls herself into his side, and she tips her head back to look up at him.

"Yes, we have a lot to do tomorrow," she tells him as Blake takes Sam from me and wraps his arm around my waist.

"We do?" He sighs, sounding unhappy, and Janet smacks his chest.

"You've had months of dealing with this alone. Get used to not being alone anymore."

"Right." He lets out a breath, and she shakes her head, then lets him go so they can both give Blake and me a hug before they leave and get into their cars.

"Are you okay?" I tip my head back to look up at him as they drive away.

"No . . . yes . . . I don't know." He lifts one shoulder. "I feel better that the truth is out, but I hate that my mom and sister are hurting now."

"I hate that for you and for them." I give his waist a squeeze. "I hope you know that I'm here for you. Whatever you need, I'm here. You can depend on me the way everyone else depends on you."

"Thank you, baby." His expression softens. "You being here is what I need. I don't know what I would've done these last few weeks without you and Sam to keep me sane." He turns me toward him and rests his forehead against mine. "I love you." He leans in to touch my mouth with his, and Sam presses his face between ours, making us laugh.

"Can we eat pizza now?" Edmond asks, and I giggle as Blake sighs.

"The pizza had to be tossed, but I'm sure I have the stuff to make some sandwiches," he tells him as he leans away from me.

"Aww, man, I was really looking forward to the pizza," he mumbles, getting off his bike, and I laugh harder, hearing Blake laugh along with me. It's that sound from him that lets me know that everything will be okay; it might not be easy, but in the end it will all be all right.

Chapter 18

EVERLY

I look over at Blake as we pull up and park in front of Tanner's house, and then I reach over for his hand. Over the last week, news of Dave's diagnosis has spread through our group of friends, and, as expected, everyone is worried. The only good thing to come out of this situation is that now, Dave has the support of his family and friends and Blake is no longer going through this alone. And even if he'll never admit it, I know that is a weight off his shoulders.

"Are you ready to do this?" I ask, and his gaze meets mine as he shuts down the engine.

"Yeah." He lifts my hand to kiss my fingers.

"I got your back," I remind him, because I know that he might have some difficult questions to answer, and with Margret things could potentially get heated, even though she's had a few days to cool down, and the last time they talked, things between them were good. I wouldn't say that she's in agreement with him keeping the secret for Dave, but I know that she understands it a little more than she did before, and more than anything, she loves her brother. And I think that everyone feels better now that Janet is on the case, making sure that Dave is doing exactly what he needs to be doing and making his health a priority right now.

"I know, but things should be cool, so don't unleash your claws just yet."

"I'll keep them tucked away for now." I laugh as he squeezes my hand before letting it go so that I can unhook my belt. When we get out, he grabs Sam while I take up the gift bag I brought over for Claire. We meet at the hood of his truck.

Before we even get up the steps, the front door opens, and Tanner steps out holding a tiny bundle in his arms with a smile on his handsome face that states clearly how happy he is.

"Hey," he says, leaning down to kiss my cheek. Then he chuckles when I pass him over the gift bag, trading him for Claire, who's fast asleep.

"She is so tiny." I touch her soft little cheek, then look at Sam when he reaches for her. "Isn't she a cute baby?"

"Cute." He looks at her, then me, and his little brows draw together into a deep frown. "My mama." He reaches for me, making all of us laugh.

"Yes, I'm your mama," I promise him. I give Claire back to Tanner before taking Sam into my arms and kissing him, which makes him giggle. As we walk into the house, I smile because before Claire was born, Cybil and Tanner's house was always in perfect order; now there's baby paraphernalia all over the kitchen counters and in the living room.

"You're here." Cybil comes down the hall, then stops to give Blake a hug before coming over to wrap her arms around Sam and me.

"How are you holding up?" I ask when she lets me go. Her eyes go to her husband, and her expression softens.

"Amazing. I mean, I wouldn't complain about having a few more hours of sleep at night, but things have been great." She looks between Blake and me. "I can't say I was surprised when Tanner told me that you two were together." I look up at Blake when he rests his hand against my lower back and wonder if I look like a lovesick fool, which is exactly what I am.

"I was surprised," I tell her as Sam reaches for Blake.

"Were you really?"

"Yes." I laugh, then turn toward the door when someone knocks. A moment later, Margret lets herself in with Taylor in her arms. As soon as Taylor sees Sam, she wiggles to get down and Sam does the same, the two of them hugging each other and rocking from side to side.

"We obviously need to get them together more often," Margret tells me before stealing Claire from Tanner.

"We're all happy to see you too," Tanner mutters, and Margret doesn't even bother acknowledging him as she carries Claire to the couch, talking quietly to her.

"We're learning quickly that we no longer exist," Cybil says, meeting my gaze. "Anytime anyone calls or texts, they only want to know how Claire is doing."

"I hate to be the bearer of bad news, but that never changes." I shrug. "Sam and I have been staying with Blake the last few days, and the only time my parents call is to ask me about Sam or to talk to him."

I walk with her into the kitchen and take a seat on one of the chairs at the island next to her. Tanner and Blake go into the living room with Taylor and Sam, who've found a ball to play with.

"Are things between you and Blake good?" she asks quietly, like she doesn't want anyone to hear.

"Given everything that's happening, yeah." I shift, feeling slightly uncomfortable, because it feels weird to talk about my personal happiness, considering what's happened with Dave and his family.

"That's good," she says quietly as she looks into the living room. "It makes a little more sense now, at least for me, why Blake has been . . ." Her words trail off, like she doesn't know what to say or doesn't want to say it out loud to me.

"A jerk?" I finish for her, and her nose scrunches. "He's had a lot on his plate these last few months."

"Yeah," she agrees, and I let out a breath. "I talked to Janet this morning. She sounded okay, but I'm worried about her."

"Me too." I glance into the living room at Blake and Margret. "I'm worried about all of them," I say, then look toward the door when someone knocks. Tanner gets up to answer it, and a second later, Maverick and Mason follow him inside, where they give him chin lifts. As soon as Taylor sees Mason, she runs to him, and he picks her up and gives her a long hug. Then he carries her to the couch, where Margret is sitting with a smile on her face. I watch the three of them together and bite my lip. I really hope that they're able to work through whatever issues or reservations they have about being together, because from the outside looking in, they look like they belong together. It's obvious that they make each other happy, judging by the smiles and soft looks they're sharing.

"You two doing okay?" Maverick wraps his arm around my shoulder in a half hug before doing the same to Cybil.

"We're good—are you doing okay?" I study him closely, wishing I knew how to read him. How he, Blake, and Tanner are so close is anyone's guess, since the three of them are so very different. Tanner is so sweet and easygoing; Blake is standoffish and tends to come across like an ass but has a heart of gold; and Maverick, even as nice as he is, is just really hard to read. Even when he's smiling, you don't know what he's thinking. The only thing I do know is that ever since his trip with Lauren and Oliver, he's seemed on edge, like he's waiting for something to happen.

"I'm doing okay," he says, then looks down when Sam comes over and tugs on the leg of his jeans. "Hey, bud." He picks him up, and Sam says something to him in his ear while pointing into the living room. "All right." He laughs as he carries him away.

"Does he seem off, or is it just me?" Cybil asks, and I turn to look at her.

"You've noticed it too?"

"Yeah, it's hard not to see that something is going on with him."

"Maybe it's everything happening with Dave; I know the guys and him are close," I say, and she gives me a look that says clearly she doesn't think that's it. "There was a girl," I add without thinking when Ozzie comes to mind.

"What?" she whispers as she leans closer to me.

"I don't know," I tell her quietly. "It was probably nothing, but I swear, ever since the time they were together, he's seemed different." She looks at him, and I do the same. "She was a client, so it's probably just my imagination, or—"

"I met Tanner on a couples retreat," she says, cutting me off. "And you work in the office at the lodge. I don't think there are rules when it comes to falling for someone."

"You're right," I agree, because I know that it doesn't matter what the situation is when you meet someone and feelings get involved.

"Well, I hope that whatever's going on with him works itself out."

"Me too," I say as Tanner and Blake both come into the kitchen.

"Should we start up the grill for dinner?" Tanner asks, looking between the two of us, and Blake slides his hand down my back.

"Yeah." Cybil looks into the living room and sees that Claire is still sleeping, and then she looks at me. "Do you mind helping me get the kabobs and salad together?"

"Not at all." I slide off my stool and go around the island into the kitchen with her. Slowly, the guys make their way outside. Margret, Cybil, and I get stuff ready while watching over Taylor and Sam, who are playing, and Claire, who's still sleeping.

When dinner is finished cooking, we all head outside and take up seats around the table, which Cybil and Tanner purchased sometime since our last get-together.

"I'd like to make a toast." Tanner lifts his beer as he glances around the table. "To friends that are more than friends and closer than family."

I pick up my glass and look around the group. When I moved back here with Sam, I had no idea how things would go for me. I just knew that with my parents' support, I'd have a shot at making a life for my son and myself. I never planned on meeting a man like Blake or making the friends I have now, but I can honestly say that I'm so grateful for all of them. They've welcomed me and my son with open arms and made us feel like we belong, even before Blake and I were together. And with Blake going through what he is, I'm even more thankful for them, because I know that no matter what happens, he, his mom, his sister, and his father have people who will be there even if times get hard.

I feel Blake's hand land on my thigh. I meet his gaze, then watch him mouth, "I love you."

"I love you, too," I whisper as I lean over to kiss him, and his lips brush across mine. I always thought I knew what it was to have a partner, but really, I had no idea, because being with someone who loves you, supports you, and is there even when things are difficult is what being in a relationship is really about. There are no words for the way you feel when you are truly loved by someone, and that's what makes falling in love so risky. I just know now that it's a risk worth taking over and over until you find the person who is meant to be yours.

Epilogue

EVERLY

As I press my lips together to keep from laughing, I listen to Blake curse up a storm while attempting to get the arch of balloons I made to stick to the edge of the window in the dining room. Tomorrow is Sam's first birthday, so everyone is coming to Blake's house to celebrate with us, but before they arrive, I want Sam to wake up to decorations like I did every birthday growing up. Even if he doesn't remember it, he'll have pictures to look back on. One day I hope it's a tradition that he shares with his kids. I know as an adult, I still look forward to my birthday because my mom always made it special for me.

"Fuck, finally." Blake looks down at me from where he's standing on top of the ladder, wearing nothing but a pair of basketball shorts, his chiseled chest and abs right there for me to admire. "Is that everything?" I look around the room at the balloons, streamers, and a banner that says **HAPPY BIRTHDAY, SAMPSON!**

"That's it for tonight."

"Good." He hops off the ladder and then wraps his arms around me. "Now I can finally have my way with you." He starts walking me backward through the kitchen and down the hall toward the bedroom, his mouth leaving a hot trail of kisses along my neck and jaw as I laugh.

"It didn't take us that long," I moan when he slides my robe off my shoulders.

"Babe, you're walking around looking like you do, wearing this." His fingers trail along the lace at the top of my breast. "I'm telling you, it took too fucking long."

"It's just a nightgown." Okay, it's a little more than that, since it's not one of my usual baggie T-shirts but instead a cute nightie that's casual but still somewhat sexy—one of six I bought for when we sleep over.

"I don't care what it is." He slides his hands up the back of it, then cups my bottom and squeezes before moving his hands up farther. He takes the nightgown with it, then tugs it off over my head. He leans back and looks down at my body, bare to him except for a pair of hip-hugger panties, then cups both my breasts. My pulse, which is already skyrocketing, speeds up even more, and the space between my legs clenches in anticipation.

Not one to miss out on the opportunity to touch him, I slide my hand down his abs and into the waistband of his shorts, then wrap my fingers around his thick, hard length. "Damn," I whisper. He groans as he drops his head back to his shoulders. Loving the power I have over him, I slide to my knees and tug down the front of his shorts, and I look up at him as I lick over the head of his cock.

"Don't play with me, Everly," he hisses as I pump him; then he curses as I suck him deep. His fingers thread through the hair at the side of my head, and his eyes stay locked on my mouth while I use my hand and mouth on him, pulling and sucking in unison. The moment I cup his balls, his cock throbs against my tongue. "Stop," he orders, but I don't. I keep going, then cry out when he pulls his hips back and hauls me up off the ground and tosses me onto the bed.

I don't even have a chance to adjust to this new position before he's tossing my panties away and spreading my legs, and his mouth is on me. Right there, right where I need him most, his tongue flicks over my clit. His fingers fill me, making me cry out in surprise and ecstasy while my back arches off the bed.

I lift my hips and slide my fingers through his hair, wanting to get closer to his talented mouth. When his lips wrap around my clit and he sucks, my entire world becomes what he's doing to me, the pull in my lower belly building, all my muscles tightening. Even knowing what's ahead, I'm not fully ready for the release as I come.

Panting for breath, Blake rubs his jaw on my inner thigh, then kisses his way up my body. He stops to pay homage to my breasts. Then, wrapping my leg around his hip, I latch onto his shoulders and look into his eyes as his hand moves between us, the head of his cock sliding between my wet folds. As he slides inside me, my breath catches and my nails dig into his skin. His mouth might be talented, but there's nothing better than being connected to him like this, being full of him, surrounded by him.

When he's fully seated inside me, he lowers his mouth to mine and kisses me softly.

"I love you," I breathe against his mouth as he slides in and out of me slowly, each thrust hitting exactly where I need it most.

"How'd I get so lucky?" He pulls back to search my face, his expression one I don't think I'll ever get used to seeing from him. I've never had a man look at me the way he does, like he thinks I'm perfect, and maybe to him I am.

As his pace speeds up, our bodies become slick with perspiration, and we cling together, kissing messily. When my core starts to clench around him, I lift up and bury my face in his neck, whimpering his name. He groans mine, then tucks his hand between us and rolls his thumb over my clit, sending me flying. His hips rock into me harder and harder; then he stills deep inside of me while groaning my name. With our hearts pounding and our chests rising and falling as we attempt to catch our breath, I kiss his shoulder.

"I want you to move in with me," he says. The panted statement catches me off guard, and I pull back so I can look into his eyes. "I know that we're still new, but I hate it when you and Sam have to go back to your parents', and even thinking about you two leaving tomorrow after his party is filling me with dread."

"Blake." I search his gaze, wanting so badly to say yes but not sure if I should. "I just . . ." I cup his jaw. "Things are good right now. What if us moving in changes that?"

"You're here all the time, baby—nothing is going to change except where you keep your clothes." He's right; for the last month, we've spent almost every night here, and things have been good. We've worked out a schedule, and it's been nice being with both him and Sam at the end of each day.

"I want you and Sam here with me. I don't want to sleep without you or wake up in the morning without having face-to-face time with Sam."

Swallowing, I nod while tears fill my eyes. "Okay."

"Yeah?" he asks quietly, sliding my hair back from my forehead.

"Yeah, I want that too. I don't like being without you, either, and I know Sam wants that too."

"Good." He rests his forehead against mine. "Now, what about us getting married and me adopting Sam?" he asks, and my heart melts while tears leak from the corners of my eyes.

"You want to adopt Sam?"

"I want you and him both to have my last name," he says quietly while swiping the tears away before they can fall into my hair. "How would you feel about that?"

"Everly and Sampson Graham, I love that—he would love that," I whisper, thinking that's the understatement of the century. Blake, even in this short time, is the man Sam has bonded with the most; he's the guy he calls Daddy and is the one he's always the most excited to see. Their bond is something beautiful, and every time I see them together, even in moments when they don't know that I'm watching, I can see how much they truly love each other. And knowing that, throughout life, this bond they share will only get stronger is something I didn't even dare to dream about.

"Then that's our plan." He kisses me and I kiss him back, wondering if it's possible for one person to be too happy.

~

BLAKE

Standing next to Sampson's high chair, with Everly leaning into my side and my arm wrapped around her waist, we listen as our friends and family sing him "Happy Birthday." A year ago, I never would have thought that this would be my life, that I would not only be in love with a woman as kind, compassionate, and fiercely protective as Everly, but that I would have a kid who might not be mine by blood but is mine in every other way. Every day since Everly came into my life, I've woken up feeling excited about the future and thankful for the family I'm building with her. And with everything happening with my dad, I'm even more aware of how limited time really is. How no moment is ever guaranteed, so you should make sure to tell the people you love that you love them and enjoy each and every second you have together. Which is why, as soon as possible, I'm going to put a ring on Everly's finger and make it so that she and Sam both have my last name.

As the song comes to an end, my mom, who's been holding Sam's birthday cake, sets it down in front of him. As expected, he digs his hands into the icing and shoves two fistfuls of cake into his mouth. Then Taylor comes over to help him out, doing the same while she stands in front of him. I look over at my sister and Mason and watch the two of them laugh. Then I smile for a different reason when Mason grabs Margret's hand and kisses it, a move that makes her face soften as she looks up at him. Another good thing to happen over the last couple of months is the two of them admitting how they feel and finally giving a relationship a shot. I won't take all the credit for them finally getting together, but I will admit that I did have a talk with my longtime friend to let him know that at the end of the day, his and my sister's happiness is all that really matters. Or maybe I should give Everly that credit, since she's the one who made me realize that my previous comments to both Margret and Mason could have been preventing them from acting on their feelings for each other.

"Ginny and Jeff are going to love these," Everly says quietly, and I look down as she holds up her phone to show me the photos she took of Sam.

"They will." I watch her send them off in a text. I kiss her temple, and she tips her head back to smile up at me. Leaning down, I brush my lips across hers, then focus on Sam when he shouts "Dada, Mama!" while holding out his hands. We both walk over to him, and while Everly kisses his cheek, I eat the cake he's offering, which makes him giggle. Looking at him and his mom, I know that falling in love with the two of them was a risk, but having what I do now, it's a risk I would gladly take every single day of my life, as long as I knew they would be waiting for me on the other side.

About the Author

Aurora Rose Reynolds is a *New York Times* and *USA Today* bestselling author whose wildly popular series include the Until, Until Him, Until Her, Fluke My Life, Underground Kings, How to Catch an Alpha, and Shooting Stars series. Her writing career started in an attempt to get the outrageously alpha men who resided in her head to leave her alone and has blossomed into an opportunity to share her stories with readers all over the world.

For more information on Reynolds's latest books or to connect with her, email her at aurororaroser@gmail.com. And to order signed books, head to www.AuroraRoseReynolds.com.

Follow her on Instagram and Twitter (@Aurororaroser) or on Facebook (@AuthorAurororaroser).